# HER DIRTY BUILDERS

## A REVERSE HAREM ROMANCE

## MIKA LANE

HEADLANDS PUBLISHING

# COPYRIGHT

Copyright© 2021 by Mika Lane
Headlands Publishing
4200 Park Blvd. #244
Oakland, CA 94602

# BE THE FIRST TO KNOW...

Want more heat, heart,
and bad boys who know what they're doing?
Join my list and I'll send the steam straight to your inbox,
starting with a deliciously naughty story:

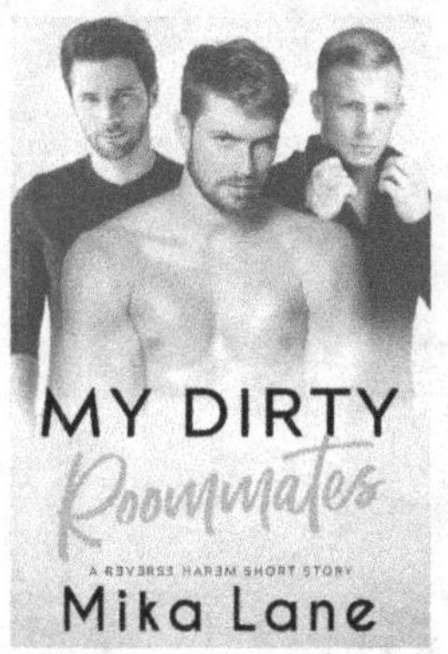


SIGN UP TO MY MAILING LIST!
Or visit:
https://geni.us/free-book-signup

## ESME RUTHERFORD

"How does my butt look?"

My best friend since forever—and if I were to be honest, lifeline to sanity—looked me up and down, the 'eleven' lines between her eyebrows more pronounced than usual thanks to her worry.

But it was all good. That's how a BFF does it. No beating around the bush. If my ass were the size of the Titanic, I'd expect her to tell me. I'd do the same.

Fortunately, my backside was *not* of Titanic proportions. But it was hefty, still. And today, the day I was wearing white, which I never did because it makes you look *big*, my butt was going to be stared at by two hundred people as they watched me walk down the aisle of a church.

To get married.

"It looks good, Esme," Charli confirmed, shaking her head. "Very bootylicious. Girls kill for an ass like yours. In fact, did you hear that women in Brazil or someplace are crazy for butt implants? I can't imagine doing that—your ass would be sore and you couldn't sit or go to the bathroom for days—"

"Charli," I interrupted, continuing to smooth my hands over my ass as if that would somehow shrink it. "I've been thinking about some things."

Her eyes widened. Guess she didn't expect a serious conversation fifteen minutes before my wedding ceremony.

"Yeah? Whatcha been thinking about, Es?" she asked, all attention, leaning against the wall of the church's dingy storage closet, which they called the 'bride's room' when they needed one.

I looked longingly at a folding chair, but we'd agreed not to sit in our dresses, at least not until we got to the reception. I'd been standing for a solid hour and was getting tired. But at least I had my shoes off.

"You know, Char... well, Eddie's really not... that into sex." I said the last words really fast and avoided her expression by studying the manicure her mother had treated me to.

She was silent. Which forced me to look up at her widened eyes.

"Oh? Really?" she croaked.

I knew that voice. It was the one she used before she broke into a panic.

"Do you… well, do you think that's a problem?" My voice was loaded with forced breeziness.

I wasn't fooling Charli, and I wasn't fooling myself.

She pressed her lips together, deliberating her words. It was not something she usually did, but considering what was about to take place, I could see she wanted to at least try to be diplomatic.

"Well, you know…" She giggled nervously. "I… um… has he been that way… all along?"

She smiled hopefully.

"Pretty much. Yeah. I told myself it wasn't a big deal. He was so nice and successful, and well, we bought the house and all, so maybe the sex thing doesn't really matter."

But for some reason it mattered *right now*, eight minutes before I was to walk down the aisle and commit myself in front of all our friends and relatives.

Damn, damn, damn.

Charli lowered her voice. "Are you getting cold feet, Esme?"

I dropped my head back and laughed hard, just to show I had my shit under control. "No, no, no," I said cheerily.

And then my bottom lip began to quiver, and the lump I'd been swallowing away for the last few days returned to my throat. My eyes filled with tears, which was disastrous, considering I'd just had my makeup done professionally for the first time in my life.

Charli rushed to me, grabbing my hands. "Oh sweetie. If you're not sure, don't do it."

"But all the people..." I said, trying to hold back a sob.

"Fuck them," she said. "This is about you. And if you don't want to do it, you don't have to."

I shook my head like that would chase away the doubts. "No. I love him. He's a good guy. I'm fine. Really. Just getting the jitters. It happens to everyone."

On any other day, Charli would call me on my shit without hesitation. But this time her mouth opened like she was about to say something, and closed just as fast. "You sure?" she asked quietly.

"Yup. I'm good."

I dug through my things for a mirror to make sure my mascara was still intact.

There was a knock on the door, and my dad poked his head in. Charli immediately stood up straight and stuck her chest out.

Yeah, she had the hots for my dad. All my friends did. He was a good-looking guy, and still pretty young since he and my mom had me when they were barely twenty.

"Mr. Rutherford. Hi," she said, batting her eyelashes.

"Charli, please call me Ben. You're all grown up now. No formalities needed."

Charli beamed.

He turned his attention to me. "Eddie's running a little late. Just wanted to give you the head's up."

I nodded. "Oh. Okay."

"You need anything?" he asked.

I looked around the room. "Maybe some water?"

He smiled, and Charli put her hand on the wall, trying to look casual.

That's how good-looking Dad was.

"I'm on it, honey. Be right back."

"It's funny that he's late. I'm usually the late one," I said once Dad had closed the door.

Charli shook her head. "Seriously. I mean, how are people late on their damn wedding day? I've never understood that. You know the date ages in advance, and you have your clothes and all that stuff picked out, so what's the holdup…"

While she ranted, I peeked out the door at the church vestibule. The arrival of guests had slowed to a trickle since it was officially past starting time.

I could call him. Maybe that's what I should do.

But that would be whiny and needy. No, he'd be here when he got here. I just had to chill.

So when ten minutes turned into fifteen, I began to get pissed. Didn't Eddie know all these people were waiting for him? And if we didn't get started soon, that would throw the reception out of whack, including the salmon, which had to be served *as soon as it was ready*. Fish wasn't the kind of thing that waited around. *You* accommodated fish. Not the other way.

"Hey, Es," Dad said, poking his head back in the room and handing me some water.

He looked serious. This was not good. Not at all.

"I think it's time we start making some phone calls." He glanced at his watch. "You know, to find out where Eddie is."

"What does his mom say?" I asked.

Dad shook his head. "I don't know. She's already seated, and I didn't want to speak to her in front of everyone."

Just then, as though she'd been summoned, Eddie's mom came flying into the room, running straight for me.

She took my hands, and her eyes were watery.

Very watery.

"Honey, I just talked to Eddie."

A single tear dribbled down her cheek.

"He's not coming."

I looked around at Charli and then Dad and laughed. "This is a joke, right? You're just pulling my leg. Eddie is so funny with his pranks."

His mom sighed. "It's not a joke, Esme. I just got a

text from him. He said he sent you a text too but that you hadn't responded."

I looked at my pile of street clothes and other crap. My phone was somewhere in that mess. That's why I hadn't gotten any text message. I ran across the room as fast as my narrow dress would let me and threw things aside until I found my phone.

His mom was right. There was a text from him.

*Sorry. Can't do it.*

"What the fucking fuck?" I screamed. "That's all I get? Four lame-ass words to call off a wedding."

My dad rushed into the room and grabbed me by the arms. "Honey, don't shout. Look, we'll take care of it."

I slipped my two-hundred-dollar high heels back on and shook Dad off. "No. You won't take care of it. And neither will you," I said, glaring at Eddie's mom.

"*I* will take care of it."

I pushed past everyone and stormed through the vestibule. I yanked open the double doors leading to the church, and walked up the aisle on the stupid white fabric thing that had been laid out for me to walk down. When I got to the front, I ignored the minister, and turned to face the congregation.

I held my phone up. "Sorry, folks. There's no wedding today. My motherfucking fiancé just broke things off OVER A TEXT MESSAGE," I shrieked.

Gasps rolled through the crowd, and people started

looking at each other in disbelief. But before they turned their attention back to me, I stormed back down the aisle and to the waiting limo.

I knew that the minute the news sank in, the next thing on everyone's face would be pity. Directed toward me.

And I was so not down with that.

2

ESME

I n   t h e   t w o   w e e k s   s i n c e   I'd   t a k e n   m y   g h a s t l y
wedding dress, stuffed it into a garbage bag, and
pushed it to the back of my closet, I'd not been doing
much more than lying around in my bedroom, stuffing
my face.

In the house that Eddie had talked me into buying
with him.

That we were going to fix up. Together. As a
married couple.

Charli had finally dragged me out my seclusion.

"Can you help me get this zipper up?" she asked,
rotating in the dressing room of her mom's very exclu-

9

sive and very expensive clothing boutique, called *To Die For*.

I wrestled the zipper of the silver sequin creation Charli had fallen head over heels in love with.

"Is that a dress or a top?" I stepped back, trying to decide.

She twirled a little, admiring herself. "Oh, it's a dress. For sure. Don't you love it?" she squealed.

"Char, I don't know where you could wear a dress like that unless it's to the gynecologist's office, because your vag is practically hanging out."

She bent to look at her crotch and the back of the dress rode up until her ass cheeks were exposed. "You have a point. It is pretty short." She looked at herself in the mirror, defeated.

"If only it were a couple inches longer," she said, tugging on its hem.

"That thing needs to be five or six inches longer before it's remotely decent."

She put her hands on her hips and tilted her head. "Hey. Why aren't you trying anything on?"

What was the point? I couldn't afford the clothes there. Charli couldn't either, for that matter. We just used the place for after-hours entertainment. With her mom's blessing of course.

A girl could dream.

I also frequently shopped online at stores like Saks

and Neiman's, filling up my cart with gorgeous things and then never checking out.

Charli wouldn't join me in this. She didn't see the point.

I picked up the clothes she'd dropped on the floor and started hanging them back up.

"I don't feel like trying stuff on. Nothing fits anyway. I've been eating too many Oreos, stressing about sending back all the wedding presents, which sounds like a total pain in the ass. On top of that, I need to figure out what to do with the house."

She wriggled out of the sequin number and took a seat in the dressing room chair. "What *are* you going to do about the house?"

That was the question weighing me down. As if it weren't bad enough that Eddie had fucked me over on our wedding day, he'd also left me with an albatross of a house.

Which he'd conveniently *never gotten around* to moving into. I'd been staying there, alone, since we closed on the house, waiting for him to find the time to bring his shit over.

A further suggestion that his bailing on the wedding was premeditated.

I buried my face in my hands. "I don't know. My dad says he'll help me get it fixed up, but I don't think he has any idea how much work the place needs. He already gave me my share of the down payment and is now out of all that money he spent on the wedding."

Thank god that when Eddie and I started planning things, I'd talked him into having his family pay for part of the wedding. I got a petty satisfaction knowing how pissed they must be at him.

I continued. "No, I'm not taking any more money from Dad. That would just be shitty, even though he says if the house gets fixed up, it could be sold at a profit."

"That's why you guys bought it to begin with, right? So you could flip it?"

"Yes, that's what Eddie wanted to do. But now he's backed out, and I don't have the money for everything that needs to be done. Well, I got a little money for my wedding, but I'm supposed to send it back, remember."

Charli and I returned all the beautiful and expensive things she'd tried to their hangers and then wandered through the store, fingering soft cashmere sweaters and silk blouses. Her mom, Francesca, had married well several times. With the proceeds from her latest divorce she walked away with enough money to embark on a 'hobby job,' opening *To Die For*, a lovely little shop despite its cheesy name. And lucky for her, it didn't really matter if she made money. The store gave her something to do with her days.

I sighed. "You won't believe this, but Dad called

McKinney Construction to get them to look at the house."

Charli stopped folding and unfolding lacy thong panties. "McKinney? Isn't that the company owned by that guy, Case? Who we went to high school with?"

It was.

And as if my life weren't messed up enough, Dad had called the one company in town run by a guy I hated.

Disgusted, I nodded. "Yeah. That asshole Case. Yuck. Can't stand him."

She tapped her forehead with a finger. "Is that the guy who…?"

She didn't finish her sentence. She didn't need to. We both knew very well who he was.

"Yes, Charli, I made out with him under the bleachers, and he went and told all his friends, who also blabbed, turning me into the school slut. Wouldn't you hate someone who did that?"

She nodded in support. "Yes. Of course. But that happened so long ago. Maybe it's time to let it go?"

Did she really just say that?

I grabbed my bag and headed for the door while Charli flipped off the lights and locked up the shop.

"You know, Es, Case McKinney was just voted most eligible bachelor in town."

No. Fucking. Way.

"Just what he needs, something else to blow up his already oversized ego."

There was no way I could work with him on my home. He wasn't the only builder in town. I'd have to find a reason not to hire him.

Well, besides the fact that he was a douche.

As we were walking toward our cars, Charli grabbed my arm and stopped me. "Es, maybe you guys will... rekindle that interest you had back then? Wouldn't that be great?"

I gave her my most devastating stink eye, then hustled to my car before I completely lost my shit.

"C'mon Es, give it a chance," she called.

I whipped around. "No. Not a chance in fucking hell."

Cripes. I'd rather let the bank come take the house and live in a tent in my dad's backyard than deal with that big-mouthed creep.

3

CASON "CASE" MCKINNEY

"Goddamn, I love Fridays."

Alden looked at me like I'd lost my mind. "Hate to tell you buddy, but it's only Thursday.

I rubbed my temples. Fuck all.

A wicked headache was circling, looking for a place to land. I took a big swig of my coffee, hoping the caffeine would stave it off.

"Right, right, right," I mumbled.

"Is something up, Case?" he asked. "You seem… drained."

I looked out my office door to make sure my mother, the office manager, hadn't arrived yet.

And then decided not to gripe to Alden anyway.

"You know, same old, same old."

I glanced up at the portrait of my dad smiling down on me and silently thanked him—for about the thousandth time—for up and dying on my mom and me and shaking up every last detail of our lives.

Especially mine.

As heir to McKinney Construction, my dad's little one-man company, I'd had to drop out of college to take over. Still didn't have my degree, which endlessly grated on me. I sucked at dealing with clients, and I had no passion for building much of anything. And I had zero time to myself. But the business was mine, and I had to work it at least until I got us out of the debt Dad left us in. *If* we ever got out of the debt dad left us in. I'd been slogging away at it for a few years now and the progress was so slow it was disheartening.

I didn't think I could feel more shackled than I did at that moment in my life. The obligations were suffocating.

I leaned back in my chair and forced myself to smile at Alden. "Just got a call. The couple we're working for across town—who fight over everything and can't make a decision to save their lives—are getting noise complaints from their neighbors about our work. Did they seriously expect construction to be quiet?"

I rifled through my dad's desk, now mine, for some aspirin.

"I don't know how my father dealt with all this," I grumbled.

Alden would know, though. He'd worked with him for years. In fact, he knew more about the business than I did. And yet, I'd become his boss.

Which was fucking crazy.

"Case, your father enjoyed this shit. He enjoyed every last bit of it. Dealing with crazy clients, flaky vendors, the permitting offices at City Hall—I don't think there was one aspect of this business he didn't get a kick out of."

"He was cut out for it. Unlike me."

Alden shrugged. "It's not for everyone. Residential building is crazy and messy. Working on peoples' homes is not for the faint of heart. There's a shit-ton of emotion involved."

Fuck. Why hadn't he left the business to Alden? He wasn't blood, but he *was* practically family. I'd been tempted on more than one occasion to hand the reins to him. But I couldn't just yet. I couldn't dump on him the mess Dad had left the place in. It wouldn't be fair to make him start with such a big disadvantage.

Alden looked at his watch. "Speaking of the feuding couple, I'm heading over there now to check on things. I'll handle the neighbors and all the other strife. Don't worry about it."

That man was a godsend.

The front door dinged as Alden left, and I started to

get some work done before my mother arrived for the day.

My phone buzzed, and while I was in no mood to chat, I grabbed for it when I saw it was one of my buddies from college.

"Phil. How are ya?" I asked.

"Hey, McKinney, how's it hanging?" he asked, yelling over the wind.

"Dude, are you in the Porsche?"

He laughed. "Yes I am, my friend. I've got the top down, and it's a beautiful day."

"You bastard."

He laughed again. "That I am."

I looked around my drab office with its decades-old furniture, framed photos of houses Dad had built, and a dusty home model some architect had left behind. I closed my eyes. What I wouldn't give to be in Phil's Porsche at that very moment.

"So, McKinney, I'm calling you again about the weekend."

I didn't realize my mood could get any worse, but it did.

"Phil, you know I want to join you guys, but the timing is just not good."

It was not only not good, it was also fucking impossible. This coming weekend—and every weekend for the foreseeable future—I'd be hunkered down with our accountant trying to piece together the shambles Dad had left the company's finances in.

My buddies were having golf weekends away, and I was holed up trying to get McKinney Construction in the black.

I hoped to catch up to my friends' lifestyles at some point—get my college degree, land a great job, and have free time to spend with them. But as every day passed, I wasn't sure that was going to happen. Like, ever.

Responsibilities. I had a mountain of them. And I'd never seen them coming.

As I ended the call, my office door flew open, initially startling me. But it could only be one person.

"Hi, Mom."

She beamed and hustled over to me. I turned my face so she could kiss my cheek and waited for her to rub my upper back before she took the seat opposite my desk.

It was what we did most every day.

"Good morning, honey. I brought you one of those scones you love." She pulled a little brown bag out of her giant tote and passed it to me.

*Yes.* I was freaking starving.

"Thanks, Mom."

She took a deep breath. "Honey, some of the ladies at my club were wondering if you could come by our next meeting and have some pictures taken with us.

You know, since you won the most eligible bachelor and all."

I groaned. "Really, Mom? I can't think of anything I'd rather do less."

She pressed her lips together and narrowed her eyes. "Look, smarty-pants. It's an honor to be voted the town's most eligible bachelor. I don't know why you're acting so put out. When what's-his-name won last year, he became quite the man about town. And… I heard from his mother that he had women *throwing* themselves at him."

Yeah, that's because the guy was a total douchebag-asshole.

"I don't want women throwing themselves at me, Mom, and I don't want to be the man about town, either. I have no time for bullshit like that."

Her head snapped back at my language. Hell if I knew why. My father swore like a sailor all his life and she'd never batted an eye.

"Furthermore, Mom, you know I'm busy with my English lit class."

She waved her hand like she always did when college came up. "Oh, honey, your father didn't have his degree, and he did just fine." She gestured around the office like it was some sort of penthouse on Park Avenue.

I counted to ten to control myself. "We've been over this a hundred times, Mom. I have different goals than

Dad's, and I will eventually finish my degree if I have to work on it till I'm forty."

God help me.

This time she held her hands in surrender. "Okay, okay. I want you to follow your dreams. Your father and I always did. But look, at least you might meet a nice girl out of being top bachelor..."

I rubbed my temples. "I don't know when I'd have time to socialize, Mom. You know I've been trying to make sense of Dad's bookkeeping so I can pay off all the vendors we owe. If I don't reduce our debt somewhat, folks will stop supplying us with what we need. Then we'll really be screwed."

She got up to head to her desk in reception where she answered phones and handled purchasing. I was pretty sure she'd contributed to the company's financial woes just as my father had. But I kept that to myself.

When she reached the door, she turned around, holding one finger up. "Oh. I almost forgot to tell you. Ben Rutherford called. He wants you to go over and take a look at the house his daughter Esme bought. You remember Esme Rutherford, don't you? You graduated in the same class?"

I shook my head slowly. I only vaguely recalled an Esme Rutherford.

"What's up with the house? What do they want done?" I asked.

"Esme bought the old Buckner house with a fiancé with the intention of fixing it up. But… he stood her up at the altar."

She clicked her tongue and shook her head with disapproval.

"And now she's stuck with it. Her father Ben feels like if they did a little fixing up, they could turn around and sell it at a small profit. You know, so all is not lost."

The Buckner house. That piece of shit? I didn't even think it was safe to enter.

The best thing to do would have been to throw a lit match at it.

"They really bought that place?"

Mom nodded. "Can you believe it? They wanted to flip it."

"Who was the guy?" I asked.

"Not sure you know him. He works for that big law firm downtown. Eddie Sanders or something."

No fucking way.

"I know that guy. He's a jerk."

Mom stood, apparently all gossiped out. "Well, maybe that's why he stood her up at the altar. Can you imagine?" she asked, shaking her head as she headed to her desk.

The Buckner house, cripes. Who the hell in their right mind would go near that dump, much less actually buy it?

Looked like I was going to find out.

4

ESME

"Nice to see you back in the office, Esme."

Twenty or so heads in the conference room whipped in my direction like I was some sort of exotic novelty. Which I guess I sort of was.

It wasn't every day you saw a woman who'd been stood up at the altar.

"Thank you, Adam," I said with my best nothing-to-see-here smile, waiting for him to move on to the next topic of discussion for our staff meeting.

But he wasn't done with me.

"I hope you had a good couple weeks off."

Really?

The only thing that kept me from leaping across the room, strangling him, and ending up in prison for life, was my fear of leaving my dad alone in this world, unable to fend off all my girlfriends who were madly in love with him.

Yeah, I ran interference for Dad on a regular basis.

I didn't want a murder on my conscience, anyway.

Amidst the stares, I hung on to my fake-ass smile. "It was lovely, Adam."

What the fuck? I had two weeks off for my honeymoon-that-never-happened, and he thought I was having *fun*?

I'd considered going right back to work after the 'incident,' but Adam had insisted I take the two weeks to 'heal' and sort out my 'emotions.'

Asshole.

Did he think I wasn't already humiliated enough without his spotlighting me in his stupid fucking meeting?

He was still pissed he hadn't been invited.

The only person from the office who *had been* invited was my work husband, Matt.

Who, thankfully, was sitting right next to me, nudging me discreetly in a show of support.

Fuck Adam for insinuating I'd had a leisurely two weeks off. I needed that time to get my head straight.

And eat.

My courtship with Eddie had been a whirlwind.

Hell, I'd only known him six months. But he came on strong, and I believed he loved me, even though Charli told me he was a bit on the smarmy side.

I attributed his eagerness for tying the knot to the fact that he was a rising star at his fancy downtown law firm and that everyone around him was married and starting families. He'd figured it was time to do the same. And I wasn't a bad catch. Not at all.

Although we *were* an odd pair—Eddie in his expensive suits and hundred-dollar haircuts, and me working at a free weekly newspaper, perpetually broke from working for pennies, and obsessed with shopping at thrift stores. But hey, it worked. Or it seemed to.

My dad had pointed out how he and my mom had been an odd pair.

And I pointed out right back how well that had worked out for them. Neither of us had seen her in ten... or was it twelve?... years.

Adam raised his voice, yanking my thoughts back to the meeting. "Remember team, get everyone you know to vote for us in the national free weekly newspaper challenge. We have a strong chance at winning, and winning will bring *City Scene* the kind of respect we deserve."

I waited for him to beat on his chest.

One of the most tiring things about Adam, and there were many of them, was that he acted like *City Scene* was the fucking *New York Times*. According to him, he'd worked there briefly as a lowly copy aide right after college, and he bitterly never stopped talking about it. He'd expected to have a career there, but for whatever reason, it hadn't panned out. No one knew why—but we could guess.

So as revenge, he was out to make *City Scene* the best paper he could, never mind that no one at the *New York Times* had ever heard of us and likely never would. He was going to show them, though. And they'd rue the day they sent him packing.

"On to the last item on today's agenda."

Sighs of relief spread through the room.

"The first annual *City Scene* retreat!" he squealed.

He looked around, expecting to see enthusiasm at least matching his.

He didn't.

"Look, guys, I know you think team-building is bogus, but this will make us a stronger and better paper."

Watch out, *New York Times*.

"And for the retreat, I'm putting Esme in charge." He clapped his hands and bounced in his sneakers a little.

Once again, all eyes were on me, and Matt nudged me hard to remind me to keep my big mouth shut. But it didn't work.

"Um, Adam, I'm really busy with setting up interviews for the women's conference coming to town.

That's going to take all my time, so maybe you could delegate this to someone else—"

But he drowned me out. "Esme will do a kick-ass job with her creative thinking and excellent organizational skills. Thanks everyone. Have a great day."

The stampede ensued as people scurried back to their desks before Adam assigned them some dumb-ass project.

Matt and I were heading to our adjacent cubes when Adam stopped me.

"Esme, can I see you in my office?" Without waiting for an answer, he turned, assuming, of course, that I would just follow.

And I did.

"Esme," he said, settling into his chair and folding his hands together, "grab a seat."

What was going on? He never invited me to sit in his office.

But I could play it cool. I settled into the chair opposite him, crossed my legs, and leaned back, the epitome of confidence with my friendly but not-too-eager smile.

"Esme, I've been thinking."

Oh god.

"You know, with your recent experience..." He paused, waiting for my reaction.

But I didn't give him one.

I could only imagine where he was going with this.

He shifted impatiently. "Well, I was thinking you could write something up for the paper. You know, about it… all. The whole thing. How it went down. How you survived it. And how you're rebuilding your life."

No, no, no.

He did *not* just ask me to write about the worst experience of my life.

How it *went down*?

How I *survived*?

Could he *be* any more demeaning?

He was probably happy when he heard the news. Figured I needed to be taken down a notch or two.

But I didn't say a word, and he continued digging himself in deeper.

"This could *really* be a hit for both you and the paper," he said smugly. "You could talk about your hopes and dreams, your dress. By the way, I heard it was very pretty."

Jesus, he *was* still bent out of shape he wasn't invited.

"Talk about the mother of the bride's dress—"

"I don't have a mother," I interrupted.

He turned a light pink. "Oh. Really? I didn't know that."

No, he wouldn't know that because all he ever talked about was himself.

He leaned over his desk with hunger in his eyes. "What do ya think?"

I hoped he hadn't noticed my hands on the arms of my chair, gripping so hard my knuckles were white. "Um, can I think about it?" I asked in a choked voice.

He smacked his hand on the desk like it was a done deal. "Excellent. Can't wait to hear your ideas."

Thank god it was time for lunch because I walked straight out of the office and to my car.

5

ESME

Not ten minutes later, I reached my house. Well, Eddie's and my house—even though I was the only one living there. I parked at the curb because the driveway was too crumbly to drive on with anything besides a four-wheel drive, and ran over the weedy lawn to the front door. I kept my gaze down so I wasn't reminded what a shithole the place was.

I was late. I was always late.

And there he was, Cason McKinney, one of the populars from high school who had fooled me for five minutes that he was interested in me.

Back in high school.

But still.

He extended his hand. "You must be Esme. I'm Case McKinney."

If it were possible, he was more dazzling than he'd been as a teenager. Damn him.

The more mature version of my one-sided interest had a couple lines in the corners of his eyes, his jawline was more defined, and his hair was tidy—an eternity away from the mop he wore in high school.

Which made me kind of sad because I loved that mop.

I returned his handshake. "Hi… Case."

I wasn't giving him the satisfaction of reminding him we'd once made out under the bleachers.

He looked around the front porch, which was badly in need of a paint job, and probably several other things. "Well, I can see right here, we have some dry rot on the porch. Probably termite issues too. Can we take a look inside?"

Shit. He'd just caught me staring.

"Oh, um, yeah," I said, fumbling with the key.

I'd refused to call McKinney Construction, so Dad had done it. I couldn't blame him. He'd put up my share of the down payment, and when I thought about it, had more right to the house than I did. But, unfortunately, my name was on the note. Along with the ex-fiancé's.

I was on the hook, big-time.

As it was, Eddie was paying the mortgage because

there was no way I could afford it. But he'd also made it clear he'd do it for a couple of months and no longer. As if he were doing me a big fucking favor.

Thanks, buddy.

Case slipped a notebook out of his back pocket and started scribbling, examining every room from top to bottom while I tagged behind, praying he'd have at least one positive thing to say about the place.

"Would you like something to drink, Case?" I asked.

He shook his head without looking at me. "No. No thanks," he muttered, and got back to his list-making.

It was a good thing he didn't want anything. I had nothing to offer, anyway.

"Hey, I heard you were voted Most Eligible Bachelor or something like that."

*This* got his attention.

"Yeah. It's true," he grumbled.

As he wandered, I followed. My skin crawled from the awkwardness of the silence.

My only solution was to fill the void.

"That must be nice. You know, to be considered a good catch. Or whatever it means."

He turned to face me. "It's really not. To be honest, it's embarrassing as hell. And now my mother's all over my ass now about finally meeting a nice girl."

*Well.* He was confiding in me.

I was breaking the ice.

"Wouldn't you like that though? I mean, doesn't every man want to meet a nice girl?"

Unless you're like my ex-fiancé, Eddie.

"I don't have time. I'm running my father's business and trying to finish my college degree. As it is, I can only take one class at a time."

Oh. Shit.

He looked over the list in his hand. "Is there some place where we could sit?"

I looked around the mostly-empty house. "Sure. There's a table and chairs in here."

I led him to the kitchen, pointing out a hole in the floorboards he needed to step over.

It was only a small hole.

"Okay. Esme. I probably don't have to tell you this house needs a lot of work."

Thanks dude, I'm not blind.

I nodded politely, keeping my snark to myself.

"The thing is, fixing this place up will probably be more than the cost of buying it."

He gave me one of those *what the fuck were you thinking?* looks. I knew it well.

"I… I'm on a pretty tight budget. Do you think we could do some cosmetic things, just enough to sell it and not lose money?"

He sighed and looked back over his list. "I suppose. What's your budget?"

"I… I don't have a budget."

His eyebrows shot up.

Yeah, I knew that sounded bad. But it was the truth.

He closed his notebook and stood. "I'm not sure I can help you Esme. I'm really sorry."

And that's when I could no longer hold in the tears. At first, they dribbled down my cheeks like big, fat raindrops, and then my face started to crumple and distort, making me even more pitiful.

His eyes widened. "Oh. Oh, I'm sorry. I didn't mean to upset you."

But it was too late. There was no coming back from my outburst. And unfortunately for him, he had to be my witness.

I buried my face in my hands to hide the mess I was turning into but knew my shaking sobs gave me away. Just as I was about to ask him to show himself to the door so I could go get some toilet paper to blow my nose on, I felt his hand on my elbow.

I looked up and saw a kindness in his eyes, like he knew what it was like when the universe decided to take a huge dump on you. It was all I could do not to tumble into his arms.

But I didn't need to. He slung an awkward arm around my shoulder and patted my arm.

And if I wasn't completely crazy, leaned over to smell my hair.

## 6

ALDEN PIERCE

"Hey, if it isn't everyone's Most Eligible Bachelor. How'd things go at the old Buckner house?"

Case rolled his eyes at me and pulled out his phone. "Here. Take a look at some of the pictures I took."

"It's a mess, isn't it?" Case's mom called from the front office.

Cripes. She wasn't kidding.

I scrolled through photo after photo of dry rot, termite infestation, water damage, and actual holes in the floorboards.

I couldn't ever recall having seen a residential project in such bad shape.

"Jesus. Did you say someone was living there?" I asked.

Mrs. McKinney showed up at Case's office door, ready with the local gossip like she always was.

"Yes, someone *is* living there, Alden. A girl Case graduated high school with. Esme Rutherford. Poor thing bought the house with a fiancé, who up and left her at the altar. Can you imagine? I mean, *can you imagine?*"

She shook her head. "I remember her from a few years back. She didn't hang out with you and your friends, did she?" she asked, looking at Case.

But before he could answer, she continued her chatter. "She was a squat little thing. Glasses and braces. Not at all pretty. But you should see her now. Quite the knock-out. I saw her wedding announcement in the paper. Wouldn't you agree, Case?"

He shrugged. "Yes, Mom, she's attractive. Now can you let Alden and me get some work done?"

She raised her hands as a peace offering then thought better of it. In fact, she walked into the office and helped herself to a corner of Case's desk, propping her behind right on it. He sighed and shook his head.

She patted my arm. "I wanted to tell you, Alden, that if Mr. McKinney were here today—god rest—he'd be so proud of you and the job you're doing with little Rose."

Case was eager to get to work, I knew, but any time

I could talk about my Rosie, I did. She was the center of my universe. "Thank you, Mrs. McKinney—"

But she wasn't done. "When that woman—I hesitate to call her Rosie's mother because a mother just doesn't leave her babies—took off, you stepped into her shoes like she was never there."

Well, yeah. What else was I supposed to do? Sit home and cry in my beer? Of course I took care of my baby. She had no one other than me.

Dammit. Every time I thought about how I was the only person in the world that Rosie had, I got choked up.

And I didn't want to get choked up at work.

"Thank you, Mrs. McKinney."

She squeezed my shoulder. "Of course, honey. Now, promise me you'll bring by the little one soon? I'm dying to see her. It's been a while."

"Sure. Maybe I'll have my mother bring her by tomorrow."

Case's mom clapped her hands together gleefully. "Oh, great!"

"Mom, if you're going to hang out with us, let me get you a chair to sit in," Case said, pulling another chair up to his desk.

"Thank you, Case," she said, settling in.

She held out her hand for Case's phone. "C'mon. I want to see the Buckner house photos, too. I'd like to know just what we're getting into."

She gasped as she scrolled. "Good lord. This reno is not going to be cheap. Or fast."

Mr. McKinney, who'd been like a second father to me, had run the business with his wife by his side since day one. While I missed the hell out of the old guy, I couldn't imagine what the loss was like for Mrs. McKinney.

I was shattered when I'd found out he was gone. It was such a shock—he'd been so healthy and robust. I guess it goes to show you never know when your number is up.

The man had given me an opportunity I doubt I'd have found anywhere else. He brought me in and taught me everything about the construction business, and treated me as an equal for the years leading up to his death.

At the time, I knew he had a son off at college, whom I'd met a couple times. But after Mr. McKinney passed and Case took over, we became friends pretty quickly. I knew Case didn't want to leave school, but he wasn't about to let his father's legacy die. He'd walked in, learned like a motherfucker, and had worked his ass off every day since.

He was a great guy. Just like his dad.

And earlier in the year, when Rosie's mom hit the road because she'd decided she wasn't *mother material*, he was totally cool about my taking some time off to make sure the baby's needs were taken care of.

And in an incredible turn of luck, my mother was willing to watch Rosie every day. What better arrangement is there? I mean, who can you trust your kid with more than your mother? Rosie might have to grow up without a mom, but her grandmother was filling that role like she was made for it. When one door closes, another opens and all that.

But that didn't lessen the sting of Rosie's mom bailing on the two of us. I'd never understand how a parent could abandon their kid. Or their partner, for that matter. There had been some dark days for a while, but I thought they were behind me now. For the most part, anyway.

"So did Case tell you his news?" Mrs. McKinney chirped.

I looked between the two of them. "What news?"

She slapped her thigh. "I knew it! He's embarrassed."

Case's lips were pressed into a thin line.

"What's going on?" I asked.

"Really, Mom?" Case started to say.

But there was no stopping her.

"Case was voted Most Eligible Bachelor," she said, beaming.

Case was not beaming. "Mom, can we not do this?" he hissed.

I held my breath to avoid laughing.

"Yeah, I heard, Mrs. McKinney. You must be so proud."

Case scowled at me again.

Mrs. McKinney waved him off. "Oh, Case, relax. Anyway, one more thing before I go. Now that I think about it, please tell me you're not taking the job at the old Buckner house. I just don't think it's a good move for the company now that I've seen those photos."

"Why—" I started to ask.

"The girl has no money," she interrupted. "We can't take on charity cases."

How did she know about the woman's financial situation? Oh wait, this was Mrs. McKinney. She knew everybody's business.

This was quite a departure from the way her husband had run the business. Bless him, he couldn't say no to anybody.

"I hear what you're saying, Mom. And maybe if Dad hadn't done so many jobs like this, we wouldn't be up to our ears in debt. But this woman is in a bind. I want to help her."

Mrs. McKinney got to her feet. "All right, Case. I don't think it's a good idea, but it's up to you. Just remember this when you turn down a profitable project for this. We all know *helping people* does not pay the bills. No matter how *pretty* those people are."

## 7

## ALDEN PIERCE

"Here's a key to the house, and my deposit."

Our new client Esme handed Case a check and me the key.

She *was* pretty. Mrs. McKinney hadn't been exaggerating. Funky too, in her old school dress and Converse Chucks.

And when Case stared at the check for a moment too long, I glanced at it and saw it was for one thousand dollars.

Guess he hadn't told her deposits are usually in *multiples* of thousands of dollars.

She smiled proudly. "I know you said no deposit

was required, but I had some money from… well, wedding gifts, and I wanted to pay you so this was a fair deal for you, too."

Crap, she was cute. So sincere and without an ounce of guile. You didn't see a lot of that in this business with all the entitlement out there. People are suspicious of builders. I guess because there are so many crappy ones, that when they do find someone to work with, they're just waiting to get screwed over. The relationship starts off on the defensive. It's a vicious cycle.

This project was… different.

While Esme and Case went on discussing it, I marveled over just how attractive she really was with her long, thick hair, curvy as shit figure, and perfect sly smile.

I hadn't dated much—correct that, at all—since Rosie's mother had taken off, but I wasn't sure how I was going to resist this woman.

And a quick glance at Case suggested he might be thinking the same. His gaze was glued to her ass as we followed her to the kitchen for coffee.

She directed us to the table, which was reached by stepping over a missing floorboard.

"Case tells me you work for *City Scene*, Esme. What an awesome paper," I said.

She turned around, her face covered in surprise.

"You read it? I'm always surprised when someone says they actually read it."

She was modest. Cool.

"You shouldn't say that, Esme. It's a great resource for what's going on around town. I always find cool things to do with my baby."

She whipped around from making the coffee. "You have a baby?"

Case rolled his eyes. He knew there was no stopping me.

"Yup. Ten months old. Red hair like mine."

I was beaming. Tough shit if anyone thought it was cheesy.

Case grunted. "Luckily, she's not ugly like you are."

Esme laughed.

"Wow. Does your wife have red hair too?"

Okay. This was the part of the conversation I didn't like.

"There... is no wife in the picture. She... took off. I'm a single dad."

Esme's eyes widened with the same expression every woman wore when they learned this about me. Why was it that people think a dude can't take care of a baby?

"Wow. That's so cool, you have a little girl. My dad raised me, too, without a mom. And look how I turned out." She rolled her eyes and laughed.

Case set down his coffee cup. I knew he wanted to get to work. "We're going to have a better idea of what needs to be done after we really dig in today. So we'll have some info for you, probably when you get home from work."

"I hope it's not too much bad news." She looked at the hole in the floor and slowly shook her head. "I mean, I'm not expecting good news, exactly. I just hope I can get a few things done and then sell the house."

She looked at us hopefully.

"Don't worry, Esme. We'll do our best to take care of you."

"I'm so… grateful," she said, hesitating.

Yeah, I'd be suspicious too.

When you looked like her, guys were always offering to do you 'favors.'

She stood, grabbing her bag off the kitchen counter. "Well. Gotta hit the road. You have my number if you need anything."

She shook both our hands and took off.

When I was sure she was gone, I looked at Case. "Dude, you can't put lipstick on a pig. What the hell do you think we can do with this place?"

He looked around the kitchen skeptically. I was happy to see he hadn't completely lost his mind.

Although he might be thinking with his little head.

"Not sure yet. But I want to get behind the water damage on that wall in the living room."

"Right. Mind if I have a look around? I want to see what we're up against," I said.

He waved his hand. "It's all yours, buddy."

I walked up the worn wooden staircase, listening for creaks to assess how solid the flooring was, when I found what must be Esme's bedroom.

It was the only upstairs room with any furniture.

And as I walked into it, something crunched under my work boot.

It was glass. Broken glass.

I looked around for its source and found what looked like a broken picture frame on the top of a stuffed garbage bag.

Lying on top was a picture of Esme with some guy. It had been yanked out of the frame, and there was heavy black scribbling over his face.

I burst out laughing. I couldn't help it. I knew how much it hurt to be left and that sometimes the silliest things helped you feel better.

I'd forced myself to keep all the photos I had of Rosie's mother, not because I wanted them under my roof but because my little girl would want them some day.

There was no crossing out faces for me. But I was glad Esme was kick-ass enough to do it.

I was going to be in trouble with this girl.

8

ESME

"*What?*"

I glanced over the cubicle wall at Matt as I reluctantly answered my cell. He gave me a thumbs down when I mouthed it was my ex-fiancé.

Eddie.

Who I'd successfully avoided until now.

"It's about time you answered my call Esme," he huffed.

To think I almost married this creep.

I lowered my voice to a whisper. "Why do you keep calling me? We have nothing to talk about," I hissed.

He sighed the sigh of an entitled dickwad who fully

51

expected people he'd fucked over to still jump to take his calls.

So clueless.

"Look, Esme. I've told you I'm sorry for what I did—"

"You told me in a *text message*."

Silence.

He had nothing to say to that. Even *he* had to know what a fucked-up thing that was to do.

"I don't want your apologies, Eddie. I'm happy you didn't show up at our wedding. You did me a favor. What I want now is for you to stop calling. I want nothing to do with you. Go fuck yourself."

Matt's eyebrows rose, and he raised a finger to his lips to remind me to keep it down.

He was right. I needed to take it down a notch. Work was not the place to have a meltdown. Even though it would feel freaking awesome.

"Look, Esme, I just wanted to talk to you about the house."

Adam wandered by, and I smiled at him. When he was gone, I returned to asshole.

"The money pit dump you stuck me with?"

"Hey, I'm stuck with it, too. In fact, since we both want to get rid of it, let's list it. Right away."

It was tempting. It really was. Just get rid of the damn thing. Eddie clearly didn't seem to mind losing out on the money he'd put into the down payment.

But I couldn't stick my dad with a loss like that, no matter how tempting it was to dump it and walk away.

"You know we'll lose money. I'm not doing that to my father."

He tapped on his computer keyboard in the background. "Esme. Do I need to remind you that I work for a big, powerful law firm? You can fuck with me all you want, but in the end, I will win."

He thought he could threaten me? If I could reach through the phone and strangle his scrawny neck, he'd be dead in minutes. "Look. The house *will* eventually be sold. I want to get some work done on it first, though, so it's not a total loss. *You* should be thanking *me* for trying to make this work for us all."

That should appeal to his vanity. If he thought I was doing anything that might remotely help him or make his life better, he was a bigger idiot than he seemed.

Regardless, I could see him shaking his condescending head on the other end of the line. How did I ever get wrapped up with him? We're so different. He was all uptight and corporate, and I was a struggling journalist who shopped at thrift stores.

I'd been over it a hundred times. I knew very well how he'd reeled me in—with his promises of love and devotion, and all that other crap I fell for like a sucker.

"Okay, Esme. Let's give it two months. We'll see what can be done to improve the place, and then we sell. But I don't know what you think you'll be able to accomplish, because *you have no freaking money.*"

He was right about that. But he didn't know I'd already engaged some very nice guys who *wanted* to help me out of this bind.

And he didn't need to know.

He also didn't need to know how freaking hot they were.

"You know, Eddie, you have a lot of nerve. You pressured me to buy the house in the first place when I didn't want to, and then you pressured me to go to Dad for my share of the down payment. And now, you've left me stuck with it. So as far as I'm concerned, you can go *fuck yourself.*"

Matt shot me a look.

Yeah, that last bit had been *loud.* I hadn't used my inside-the-office-voice. But who could blame me? My coworkers all knew the recent shit I'd been through, and I was sure none of them would deny me the pleasure of screaming at the fucker who'd messed up my life.

Not to mention they were gossipy as hell and loved something juicy to talk about.

"Eddie, I need to get back to work. Goodbye," I said, swiping the call over.

Not that getting rid of Eddie was much better than the task that lay before me—planning the stupid office retreat. Everyone wanted something different, and they were all over me to accommodate them.

Reasoning with Eddie or trying to make everyone in the office happy—which was the more cruel, thankless job?

Especially when I had real work to do, like cover the women's conference that was coming to town.

"Matt," I whispered over the cube wall.

He spun around in his chair to face me. "What's up?"

"The retreat."

He raised his eyebrows. "What about it?"

I leaned over the waist-high cubicle wall so he could hear my lowered voice. "It's a pain in the ass. I can't give everyone what they want. They're going to hate me."

He rolled his eyes and turned back to his laptop, where I was pretty sure he was writing about the surprise closure of the oldest bar in town. "Fuck 'em," he said over his shoulder.

Well. He was of no help. And Adam wasn't around, having gone out to impress the paper's parent company that he needed a bigger budget or something like that.

And I had no doubt he was dropping names all over the place of the people he'd worked with so long ago at the New York Times.

Now that I was mad at the world, I figured it was time to leave work before I hurt someone.

**I headed home to see what was going on there.**

## 9

## ESME

WHILE I DIDN'T WANT TO LOOK A GIFT HORSE IN THE mouth, I couldn't help but wonder why Case was being so kind and polite. It was pretty clear he didn't remember me from high school, which was probably for the best, but he'd been such a douchebag back then, making out with me and then blabbing to his stupid jock friends.

When had he become a nice human being? Was it just plain old growing up? Or had life done something to humble him?

I pulled up in front of my house to find the guys

still there. And the house was still standing. So there was that.

Thank god. I needed something positive in my life.

But that brief sensation of having things under control like a normal, competent adult withered when I walked inside and saw the gaping hole in my living room wall.

With bits of plaster and wood crunching under my feet, I slowly made my way toward it as if it might swallow me up.

"What the hell?" I yelled, fingering the edges where the old plaster and wood had been pulled away.

Behind where the wall had been, there was another wall.

Completely made of brick.

I didn't know much about home construction, especially not old houses, but I didn't think this was normal.

Goddammit. A sledgehammer and other tools of destruction lay scattered around the floor amidst the debris. Did the guys do this? And why?

"Oh, hey, Esme. We were just getting ready to head out for the day," Case said, smiling as he and Alden found me.

They were covered in dust. My dust. My *wall* dust.

"What... what is this? Why is there a hole in my wall?" I stammered.

He pointed. "Oh that? Yeah, we were looking for a source of the water damage, and look what we found."

I looked at them, the mess on the floor, and the hole. Did they see something I didn't? Because I was pretty sure a huge hole was a huge hole.

"What? What did you find? Because it made a big fucking mess in my house!" I shrilled.

The two guys looked at each other, puzzled.

"Well, that. Right there," he said, continuing to point.

Oh my god.

I unclenched my teeth and took a deep breath. "What is that? What are we looking at?" I asked with all the patience I could muster.

Because all I could see was the goddamn hole and trash all over my floor.

Did I need to remind them that the goal of this project was to improve the house, not to waste time trying to discover its secrets?

"Check it out, Esme," Alden said, putting his hand through the new opening and reaching for the brick inside.

"What is it? Why is there brick behind my wall?"

Alden smiled. "It's not just brick. It's an old fireplace. Someone covered up a fireplace."

While I supposed that was interesting and even a bit mysterious, I didn't feel better about it.

"We occasionally make interesting finds like this

with old houses. It tells you about its history, and the people who inhabited it at one point," Case added.

They were clearly pleased with themselves.

Me, not so much. I mean, I was glad they were intrigued. I was happy that their day had been made more interesting.

But mine had not.

In fact, all I could think about now was that there was a hole in my wall where there was none before. And that meant my house—and I—had another problem.

"I… I think you guys better leave now. I need some time to myself," I said, choking back tears.

They looked at each other again. "Um. Okay. See you tomorrow, then." They grabbed their things and left.

And thank god they did because that's when the flood came. I sank down to the floor, surrounded by bits of wall and put my head in my hands, the sobs coming hard and fast.

I hadn't meant to be such a bitch to the guys. But at that moment, it was like something came over me. I wanted someone to blame my problems on, and they were in the wrong place at the wrong time.

I reached for the handle of the sledgehammer and dragged it closer. It was freaking heavy, so I got to my feet for leverage in picking it up.

I held it in two hands and when I swung it, it nearly

pulled me over. No wonder it was so good at breaking shit.

I swung it again, this time against the remaining part of the living room wall that the guys hadn't gotten to. The sledgehammer exploded against the wall, and big chunks of plaster crumbled, followed by the wooden lath it was attached to, revealing more brick.

It was actually kind of fun.

So I swung it again and again until I was coughing from the powdery dust and my eyes burned. It was only when I began to choke that I threw down the sledgehammer and waited for the air to clear.

Just when I was thinking I'd surely helped the guys with their demolition work, I looked up to see a crack extending from what was left of the wall, across the ceiling. That hadn't been there before.

Neither had the big sag overhead. Nor the cool breeze now blasting into the room.

Shit.

I ran to my room and went to bed, pulling every blanket I had over me to keep warm.

The only good news was that the guys were coming back in the morning, and if I froze to death overnight, at least they'd find me.

## 10

## TY WELLS

"WELL, WOULD YOU LOOK AT THIS PLACE?"

I bounded up the steps of the old Buckner house, hoping my work boot wouldn't crash right through the flimsy floorboards.

Alden put his hands on his hips and looked up at the sagging porch roof hanging over our heads and nodded.

Had I brought my hard hat? I didn't usually wear them for residential construction, but it might be time to start.

"Yeah, it's something, isn't it?" he said, shaking his head in disbelief.

Case did the same. "We figured we'd hang out here on the porch waiting for you until the last possible moment because the interior is so… well, you'll see," he said with a grimace.

"Who the hell bought this place?" I asked.

Case shook his head. "A very unfortunate person, that's who. C'mon, let's go inside."

"Don't forget to add that she pretty much read you the riot act last night so bad we practically ran out the door," Alden said with a laugh.

Oh shit. One of *those* clients. I didn't need that sort of drama. I had enough of my own.

He took the key and pushed open the front door. I followed the guys in and we all stopped dead in our tracks.

"What the fuck?" Case said.

The living room was trashed. Almost one entire wall had been torn away, and the floor was covered in remnants of it. To make matters worse, the missing wall must have been load bearing, because now the ceiling drooped, and a cool breeze ruffled through the room.

"Oh no. Did she take up the sledgehammer after we left last night?" Alden said.

Nothing worse than a do-it-yourselfer trying to 'help' the job along.

Case picked up the sledgehammer from the floor and leaned it against the wall. "I'm gonna sweep this up before someone gets hurt on the mess," he said, picking up the big push broom in the corner.

"What's going on here, guys? Can someone fill me in? Was the house already like this?" I asked.

"Case and I started demoing the wall to check for water damage and found this old fireplace behind it. I guess a previous owner didn't like it, and it was cheaper to just build a new wall."

It was crazy, the things you came across in an old home. There were always surprises.

"Okay, so you demoed this wall. Why'd you make such a big fucking mess?" I asked.

Case had gotten most of the debris shoved out of the way and into a corner. "We did not make this big fucking mess. It was a *little* mess when we left last night. Draw your own conclusions."

"No shit. The client did this?"

Done with the broom, Case looked down at the floor, shaking his head. "Maybe my mother was right. Maybe we shouldn't have taken this job."

Alden filled me in. "The owner, Esme, recently had some drama in her life—"

"She was left at the altar," Case interrupted.

Ah-ha. That would push anyone over the edge.

"We wanted to help her out because she's kind of broke with the fiancé bailing and all," Alden added.

"But if she's going to be a pain in the ass about

things, we don't need the headache," Case said, pulling out his cell phone.

"I'm calling her right now," he added.

Alden and I looked at each other. This could get ugly. I'd seen Case pissed before. He didn't have the patience of his father.

"Hello, Esme? Case McKinney here."

Once they got past their pleasantries, Case got to the point.

"Esme, did you take the sledgehammer to the wall here after we left last night?"

Why was he asking her? It wasn't like there was anybody else who could have done it.

"Well, you shouldn't have done that. You just made our job a lot harder."

I looked over at Alden, who was trying not to laugh. Of course, that brought me to the brink of laughter, too, listening to Case scold a woman who was probably already mad at the world.

"I know... I know, Esme. Look—"

Alden and I were shaking with laughter, listening to Case try to get a word in edgewise. If he thought he was going to set that woman straight, looks like he had another think coming.

But then he raised his voice. "Esme. I am trying to help you here. We all are."

There was a long pause.

I hoped he hadn't gone too far. But if he had, it

didn't seem like it would be a huge loss, if this wasn't going to be a money-making endeavor, anyway.

On the other hand, being able to say we'd renovated the old Buckner place would surely be a nice feather in the cap of McKinney Construction. And from the looks of the place, while it definitely needed shoring up, it had good bones. I'd love to get to work on restoring some of its original wood.

Case lowered his voice and wandered off to another part of the house, either for privacy or possibly to get away from our smart-assed laughing.

"Are you okay, Ty? You look a little tired," Alden said.

Shit. Did I look that bad?

"Oh, yeah, I was arguing with the old man again last night. That takes it out of me. He's hammering me on my career choices. The thing that's ridiculous though, is that no matter what I did, it wouldn't make him happy."

So I might as well do what the hell I wanted.

Alden slapped me on the back. "Sorry to hear it, man. It's a shame he doesn't see the value in your woodworking talents."

Truth be told, he didn't see value in anything about me. I think the thing he liked best was calling on a regular basis and dumping his shit all over my head.

While we were waiting for Case to finish with the homeowner, Alden and I wandered to the kitchen. It, like the rest of the house, was a mess, but nothing that some hard work—and unfortunately, a big chunk of money—couldn't repair.

"You know, these cabinets could be fixed up with some refinishing and new doors. They'd look great," I said.

And even better with brand new ones.

I knew Case and Alden thought the house was beyond hope, but I didn't see it that way. From my perspective, wood had many lives and could be repaired, reshaped, and refinished until there was nothing left but sawdust. That's what was great about these old places. They were made out of strong building materials. Most anything could be brought back to life.

"Okay, guys," Case said, putting his phone back in his pocket and joining us, "I don't think Esme will be breaking down any more walls."

Alden snickered. "What did you do? Remind her you're the most eligible bachelor in town?"

Case glared at him. "Very fucking funny, man."

I looked between the two of them. "Wait. What? You got Most Eligible Bachelor this year?" I dropped my head back and let out a whoop that echoed through the house.

Without waiting for him to answer, Alden continued his ribbing. "I know right? Who'da thought this ugly mug would get voted anything?"

"Is our new client Esme bewitched by your special status?" I had to add to the ribbing. It was just too tempting.

"Hardly. I'm sure she thinks I'm an asshole, after the conversation we just had," he said, pulling out a notebook.

Alden shrugged. "Great. All the more for me."

Our gazes snapped in his direction.

"*What?*" he said, holding up his hands and shrugging. "She's freaking gorgeous. And if she thinks Case is a dick, so much the better for me."

"I thought you were off dating since Rosie's mom took off," Case said.

Alden shrugged playfully. "I might be. And I might not be. But hey, I'm not selfish. I can share."

## 11

## TY

"Esme. Good to see you again."

I'll be damned. I already knew this woman. Sort of.

She stopped making coffee long enough to put a hand on her hip and returned my shake. "Nice to meet you, Ty. You do look familiar."

Her smile was dazzling. A little crooked and perfect at the same time.

"You work at that newspaper, right? The one in the old elevator building?" I asked.

"*City Scene*? Yes," she said, still trying to place me.

I knew it. "I was recently doing some work there restoring the original beams."

Her eyes opened wide as she remembered—or at least pretended to. "Right. *Yes*. You did an awesome job. I love that building and all its industrial chic."

She laughed, and I found it hard to look away. Case might have had it out with her, but she was lovely. I could listen to her laugh all day.

I'd noticed her right off the bat at the paper during my job there a month earlier. I was usually pretty heads-down when doing my thing, especially in a place of business, not wanting to be disruptive. But with this one, well, I couldn't help but notice her joking and laughing with her coworkers. She was like a ray of light.

And it didn't hurt that she was fucking beautiful. Long, thick hair and flawless skin. Funky dresses that looked like they'd come from a vintage shop.

So different from the kind of women I usually met, or who my parents tried to introduce me to.

"And here comes Case," she teased as he joined us in the kitchen. "I think this guy here would prefer I leave the home renovations to him. Can't say I really blame him."

Case raised his eyebrows at her, grinning devilishly. He was no dummy, and he knew when he was being goaded. But I also knew he could give as well as he could get.

"Well, Esme, if you hadn't made such a mess, I wouldn't have had to spend half the day cleaning it up.

So I'd say stick to your newspaper work, and we'll stick to building."

"If you'd just let me know the whole wall didn't need to come down," she said in retort, "I wouldn't have wasted my time helping—"

"*Helping*? That's what you call that disaster? *Helping?*"

I stepped between them and raised my hands like I was breaking up a kids' fight. "All right, everybody. Let's take it down a notch."

Esme was trying not to laugh. Fuck, she was cute.

"So, Miss Homeowner, why don't you show me around the house?" I asked.

"Okay, right this way, Mister Woodworker."

I followed, and damn if my eyes weren't burning into her luscious backside as she climbed the stairs to the second floor.

"There are four bedrooms up here, all pretty small. You know back when they built houses like this, they chopped everything up into small rooms. If I had unlimited funds," she paused long enough to laugh and roll her eyes, "I'd love to combine a couple of the rooms into one master bedroom and add a bath or something."

I dug how she saw the possibilities. It was just too bad this was a quick turn-around project where we were doing mostly cosmetic stuff. But the next owners could be ambitious if they wanted to.

"And here is my room," she said, leading me into a surprisingly nice set up considering the condition of the rest of the house. "My dad came over and did a couple things so the room was livable."

She had a girly cast-iron bed with a thick, white comforter and like most women, a shit-ton of throw pillows. Her dresser was covered in an assortment of framed photographs and scented candles, and there was an empty wine glass on her nightstand. It was all pretty routine until I wandered over to her bookcase and saw a big old vibrator on top of a bunch of paperbacks.

I quickly turned back to her, pretending like I hadn't seen anything.

"Hey, look at this little jewelry box," I said, directing her attention to the other side of the room. I lifted the lid and one of those tiny ballerinas started to twirl, accompanied by tinny music.

"Oh yeah. I've had that since I was a kid. It's kind of juvenile, but also sort of retro, I figure."

Without thinking, I picked it up. "My sister had one just like this." I ran my fingers around the box's edges.

"Oh yeah?" Esme asked. "Does she still have it?"

I set it back down before I dropped it. The mention of my sister often caused a grinding pain in my stomach. I never should have brought her up.

"Um. Well, she's deceased, so not sure what happened to hers. Happened a couple years ago now."

I stared at the jewelry box so I could avoid looking at Esme. I knew her eyes would be full of pity, and I'd had enough of that for a lifetime.

But when she moved closer, she placed a hand on my arm, and I could no longer avoid her gaze.

And I was glad I hadn't. Instead of pity, her eyes were full of support. As if she were saying, 'I got you.'

Wow.

Without thinking, I leaned closer to her and brushed my lips over her temple.

And just as quickly, I pulled back.

Shit. Why had I done that?

"Hey, it's been a long day," I said, moving toward the door. "Guess we'd all better head out so you can relax and enjoy your evening."

She seemed unfazed by my almost-kiss. Unlike me.

"Oh, I'm heading out in a bit, anyway. Going to meet my friend Charli for a drink."

Damn. She'd just been left at the altar and already had a new guy? It wasn't surprising, I guess. She was pretty cool.

Looks like I'd missed out.

12

———————

ESME

"Oh my god, Es, have I got news for you."

I was grabbing the bar stool next to Charli when she gripped my arm with two hands.

"Ouch, that hurts, you know," I told her.

She released me. "Oh. Sorry. You know how I get excited about things."

I ordered a beer from the bartender, which caused Charli to wrinkle her nose. It always did.

"You know—" she started to say.

But I cut her off. "I know. I know I should drink martinis like you. But I don't like them. And I don't care, Charli. And sometimes I just feel like having a beer."

She rolled her eyes in disbelief. "Whatever."

"So what is your crazy news? You have sex with another guy in your mom's store?"

"Shhh," she said, looking around. "You never know when my mom might join us."

"Is she joining us? I'd love to see her."

Charli shook her head. "Doubt it. I think she's got a date with a man who owns a private plane."

Francesca, Charli's mother, had more dates than Charli and me put together. I aspired to be like her someday—in her fifties and still in huge demand.

"Anyway, the news is about Eddie."

My beer suddenly didn't taste that great.

"I really don't care to know anything about that asshole—"

"He's already got a new girlfriend," she blurted, slapping her hand on the bar loudly enough for heads to turn.

Now my stomach didn't feel that great, either.

I didn't want to hear about Eddie. Ever. And I especially didn't want to hear I'd been replaced so quickly.

I watched the bubbles in my beer bounce around and then downed what was left in the glass.

Fuck, fuck, fuck.

I didn't hate Eddie. He wasn't worth hating. But it

did not feel good to hear Charli's news. He already had a new woman? Such total bullshit.

And I knew what else that meant.

"I bet he was seeing her while we were engaged."

Charli opened her mouth to say something, but stopped.

She couldn't fool me.

"What? Look, you've already spoiled my night, so you might as well give me all the dirt," I insisted.

She grimaced. "I shouldn't have said anything. I can never keep my mouth shut, can I?"

I shrugged a shoulder. "Don't worry about it. I'm not."

I might not hate Eddie, but I did think he was a complete and total asshole, especially for leaving me to deal with the house *he'd* wanted so badly.

Another serious dick move.

He'd pressured me to go to my dad for my share of the down payment when he could have managed the whole sum himself. He'd said that wouldn't be *fair* to cover the whole thing himself.

There wasn't anything fair about how things were going, now, was there?

"C'mon. Spill it," I insisted.

"Well, you were right. The other girl was in the picture before he… flaked on the wedding." Her voice trailed off as if that might ease the impact.

It figured. Just figured.

But I wasn't going to let a little bad news ruin my night. I had three hot men working on my house. And, if I weren't mistaken, just this evening, one of them had sort-of kissed me.

The gorgeous Ty, with towering height and blond man bun.

So take that, universe.

"Fuck this," Charli said, laying money on the bar. "Let's go over to my mom's shop and try stuff on."

I wasn't really in the mood for *To Die For*. But I also wasn't in the mood to let Eddie the asshole invade my thoughts.

Maybe we *should* go try on some things we couldn't afford. Charli had been talking about starting an Instagram with photos of the two of us wearing things from her mom's shop.

Francesca didn't mind us playing dress up with her things, but she'd always been clear that we were never, ever to wear anything outside the store. Unless we paid for it first.

And the likelihood of that was pretty low.

"All right. Let's head out," I said, waving goodbye to the bartender

"Esme? Esme, is that you?" a deep voice said from behind me.

I whipped around to find Alden standing there, wearing a surprised smile.

Jesus, he was cute with that red hair and dimpled

chin. I'd never found ginger guys to be hot, but then I'd never seen one quite like Alden—broad shoulders, big biceps, narrow waist, and flat tummy. What was there not to like?

"Oh my god, Alden, what a surprise. Hi. This is my friend Charli."

As the two shook hands, Charli didn't let go. She also batted her eyelashes and pushed her boobs out, just like she always did with my dad.

"And how do you two know each other?" she asked, no longer interested in running over to her mother's shop.

I lightly touched Charli on the shoulder to try to get her to stop staring. "Alden is part of McKinney Construction, the builders fixing up the house before we put it back on the market. Because, you know, it's doubtful there's another sucker out there besides me who would buy the place in the crappy condition I did."

Charli finally released poor Alden's hand, and he stuffed it in his pocket as if she might grab them again.

"Let me get you ladies a drink," he said, waving the bartender over.

Charli clapped her hands. In addition to trying on stuff at her mom's shop, she loved nothing more than a party. "Tequila. Let's get tequila," she squealed

"You heard the ladies," he said to the bartender.

"So what brings you here, Alden? Don't you have to be home with your baby?" I asked.

"Oh my god. You do *not* have a baby," Charli gushed.

I could almost hear her ovaries doing backflips.

He beamed, which was beyond enchanting. "I do have a baby. Little Rosie." He pulled up a photo and passed his phone to Charli. "She's home with my mother, so every now and then on my way home from work, I swing by here for a drink. The bartender is an old friend of mine."

Charli silently passed Alden's phone to me, and I could immediately see why she was at a loss for words. Rosie was a chubby-cheeked little human with the beginnings of bright red hair the same color as her father's.

Delicious. There was just no other word.

"Amazing," I said, handing the phone back.

He stared at it for a long moment, as if he couldn't quite believe it himself. "Thank you," he said quietly.

"So where is Mrs. Alden?" Charli asked hopefully.

I'd have to talk to her later about the advantages of subtlety.

Alden's face darkened as he reached for his tequila shot. "I actually couldn't tell you. She split a few months ago. It's just me and my girl now."

I raised my shot glass. "Here's to the beautiful baby Rosie."

He relaxed a little, and we threw back our tequila.

Before long, one shot turned into three for Charli and me. Or was it four? Alden, who'd wisely stopped after one, offered to drive me home when Charli called an Uber.

When I stood from my barstool, he caught my arm to steady me. "Okay, cowgirl. Let's take it easy."

I leaned onto him. "I'm sorry. I shouldn't have had that much to drink. I'm going to regret this tomorrow."

The cool glass of Alden's passenger side window felt good on my face during the quick ride home. "Thank you for working on my house, Alden. I know you guys are really trying to help me. I appreciate it."

He turned onto my street and pulled up in front. Even in the dark, the place looked like a dump.

"Alden—" I started to say. But when my hand brushed his, a jolt shocked me to my core.

I wasn't sure whether I was more surprised about his hand touching mine, or my visceral reaction to it. But it didn't matter. Before I knew it, he leaned toward me until his lips touched mine, soft and warm.

I wanted more.

So I put my hands on the sides of his face and melted into him.

## 13

## ESME

"Hello, this is Esme."

I knew better than to answer a strange number on my phone, and yet I went ahead and did it anyway.

Did it have something to do with the time I'd spent with Alden the previous night, and my not-so-subconscious hope that he was thinking about me like I was him?

And that maybe he was calling me?

Such hopes were quickly dashed.

"Miss Rutherford, this is Mr. Darling."

Mr. *Darling?*

"At the bank. I'm calling about your overdue mortgage payment."

Oh. *That* Mr. Darling.

Wait a minute. Overdue mortgage payment? Wasn't Eddie taking care of that?

As hard as it was with the rage that began to bubble inside me, I calmed my voice. This was one conversation in my cubicle I didn't even want my work husband to hear. But as soon as I started speaking quietly, Matt turned around, curious.

Because of course.

"Mr. Darling, have you called my former fiancé, Eddie Carmichael? Until we sell, he's supposed to pay the mortgage."

And if he *were* paying the mortgage, would the bank be calling me?

What the fuck. Did Eddie just wake up some morning and think 'what can I do to endlessly make a mess out of Esme's life?'

"You can be assured we did call him, Miss Rutherford. But we can't seem to catch him on the phone. Since your name is on the note, you're responsible, too, you know."

Yeah, I knew that. Thanks, buddy.

I gripped my red stapler. It would feel so good to chuck it through a window. But that would be one more thing I'd have to fucking pay for.

"Okay. Let me get in touch with him and get this straightened out. I'll get back to you." I ended the call.

Goddammit.

I put my head in my hands. I didn't care who in the office saw my distress. Might as well still milk the stood-up-at-the-altar thing. Hell, even the morning muffin guy had been leaving me a freebie every day.

The warm, juicy feeling of having kissed Alden the night before evaporated about as quickly as it had come on.

I tried to latch on to it for a little longer.

One moment I'd been getting a ride home thanks to too many tequila shots, and the next, I was making out with him in front of my house.

"You're very pretty, you know," he'd said, pushing hair out of my face.

Holyshitholyshit.

The way this gorgeous man, with his fiery hair and chin dimple, brushed his lips down the side of my neck was hypnotic. My eyes fluttered closed, and I arched to give him better access.

"Tastes so good…" he murmured, his breath warm and smelling faintly of expensive alcohol.

I reached for his shirt and began wrestling with the buttons. I had no idea where I was going with things, but I wanted to touch him, and the moment I ran my hands over his hard pecs, I was transported away from my dumpy house and asshole boss and to a place where pure desire ruled.

In that imaginary place, I was beautiful, and everything around me was, too.

But Alden's phone buzzed a minute later, and he grabbed for it, extricating himself from me. "Hey, Mom. I'm heading home soon."

Oh. Mom.

Buzzkill.

"Yeah, I'll pick up some milk. See you in fifteen," he said, swiping his phone closed.

Shit. I could have made out with this man all night long. So I started buttoning his shirt back up. I figured it was the least I could do.

He laughed and took over. "No worries. I got it."

"Well, if you're sure, I'll let you get home. Thank you again for the ride and the... tequila."

Like the nice guy he was, he waited for me to get into the house before he took off.

And now, not twelve hours later, the wind had been sucked out of me so hard I felt like I was choking.

I dialed my dad.

"Hi, honey."

He never failed to pick up my calls on the first ring. No matter what he was doing. It was amazing. I knew I was fortunate.

Lucky on the dad front. Not so much the mom.

"Dad, the bank called. Eddie has not been paying

the mortgage." I tried to steady my voice but it wobbled, nevertheless. It always did when I heard his kind voice.

"Are you kidding?" he said. "What is wrong with that man?"

He sighed.

Eddie didn't care that by fucking me over, he was also fucking my father over. And that made me madder than anything.

My dad was not a rich man. He'd worked his way up from warehouse worker back in the day to where he was a manager now. He'd done well, especially considering the company had been jerks about the fact that he had no college degree. He'd saved money for my college, making one sacrifice after another to make up for my absent mother. It wasn't easy on him. I knew over the years he'd wished for a partner, but kept women he dated at arm's length on my account.

Now that I was older, I hoped he'd find someone. It wasn't like there was any shortage of women interested in him.

"What should I do?" I asked. "About the house?"

He took a deep breath. "You have to get in touch with Eddie. The two of you will figure something out. And you could also consider looking for a higher-paying job somewhere. You can't keep working at the paper for pennies. I know you love it there, but you need to be able to support yourself. Obviously."

It hurt to hear that. He'd always supported my journalistic dreams.

I knew he meant well, but I couldn't help but feel crapped on.

But I could deal.

I'd get rid of the house faster than I'd planned.

Which was totally possible because I had three guys on my side to make exactly that happen.

## 14

CASE

"CASE, HONEY, I HAVE SOMETHING TO TALK TO YOU about."

I looked up to find my mother in my office doorway. I don't know how my father ever got anything done.

Maybe that's why the company was in the shape it was.

"Hey, Mom. What's up?"

"My friend Lois called me the other day."

Lois... which friend was that? The one from the gardening club? Or cards? I couldn't keep track.

My mother had a more active social life than anyone I knew.

"Oh yeah? How is she?" I asked, knowing that showing interest in her friends made her very happy.

But she did that raise-one-eyebrow thing she always did before she dropped a bomb.

I did not have time for this.

"She's quite upset with you."

What? *Me?*

"Do I know her, Mom? And why would she be upset with me?"

I looked at the quote on my computer that I was working up for a new client. One that would pay. A great deal of money.

I might like helping out a pretty girl like Esme with her money pit house, but I still had to pursue paid work.

And my quote was due in an hour.

"Case, it seems you took her daughter out recently."

"You mean Camille Vale? Lois is her mom?"

Camille Vale. Hadn't thought about her since the night we went out. For good reason.

"Yes, Lois is Camille's mother." Mom strolled over to the large framed photo of my father, and stared at it with reverence.

Then she turned to face me with narrowed eyes. "Apparently, Case, you slept with Lois' daughter and then never called her again."

Holy shit. Why did I suddenly feel like a fourteen-year-old boy getting caught jerking off?

And did women really tell their mothers when they fucked a guy on the first date? I thought if you were old enough to do shit like that, you were old enough to keep it from your mommy.

I guess that didn't describe Camille Vale. And when I thought about it, I wasn't surprised.

However, I'd never expected our night together to come back to haunt me.

"It's true, Mom."

I wasn't going to lie about it. We were all consenting adults.

Mom looked down and shook her head slowly like I'd done something to disgrace the family name.

"As you can imagine, I was very embarrassed," she sniffed.

Note to self… check next date for overly strong mother attachment

"Embarrassed about what? That your grown son had sex?"

Christ, she should be happy for me. I'd just broken the dry spell from hell. And I wasn't one to discuss my sex life with my mother, but since she'd brought it up…

"If you want to know the truth, Mom, Camille was great. The evening was a lot of fun, especially when we got back to her place—"

She held a hand up to stop me.

"—but the minute she started talking about how she wanted to get married, she ruined the whole vibe."

Mom sniffed. "Well, both Lois and I think that's a terrible thing to do, and that you owe Camille an apology."

Was she serious?

It was one thing that my mother had pressured me to take Camille Vale out on a date. I really hadn't wanted to, but Mom had explained she owed Mrs. Vale a favor.

Yup. My mother was pimping me out.

But it was another thing entirely that she thought it was okay to get into the business of my sex life.

Such as it was.

"Okay, Mom. Let's do this. If you agree not to try to fix me up with any more of your friends' daughters, I promise not to have sex with them and never call again. Do we have a deal?"

Her lips pressed into a thin line as she glared at me.

I was pretty sure she'd be staying out of my love life after that.

Jesus, I hated being fixed up, and I hated even more being fixed up by my mother. It wasn't that Camille Vale hadn't been a nice woman to spend an evening with. She was smart, attractive, and a successful lawyer. We'd enjoyed a couple drinks, and gotten a late bite to eat. She invited me back to her place, a beautiful, modern condo on the top floor of a new building. I was all in.

And I might even have asked her out for a second date, not that I really had time for that sort of thing, except, during our post-fuck cuddle, she started on what I called 'the marriage talk.' There wasn't much that chased me away faster than a woman who went down that road.

It just rubbed me the wrong way. Like she was testing me. I was waiting for her next inquiry to be about how much money I made.

So that was the end of that.

And two weeks later I was getting shit over it.

I had enough problems in my life.

Hell, just the previous week, I showed up at the home of a potential client who needed to have her roof replaced.

But when I arrived, she answered the door in a sheer robe and a lacy thong.

I explained I'd come back when her husband was home.

Had my dad gone through this shit?

## 15

# CASE

I WAS RUNNING SOME QUICK ERRANDS BEFORE I SPENT the rest of my down time on schoolwork when I spotted Esme coming out of the local card shop. I was too far away to say hi, and thought better of hollering across the street. I figured I'd watch her for a bit.

Yeah, it was borderline stalkerish, but I was curious about her, and couldn't figure out why I didn't remember her from high school. She seemed like just the kind of girl I would have liked.

She must have been on her lunch hour, because I knew we were close to the renovated building where elevators had once been made. I remembered what a dump the abandoned place had been when I was a kid, and to see it now, all spruced up and full of businesses, well that made any builder like me sing. We loved seeing new life breathed back into our work.

With a small shopping bag in hand, Esme wove through the lunch-hour pedestrians, long hair whipping around her face, cute as hell in her funky dress and clean white sneakers.

She still wasn't especially warm to me, and while I wasn't entirely sure why, I was happy to be helping her fix up the house that she should never have bought. It was a shame she didn't have the budget for us to really tear into the place. It certainly had the potential to be the gem it once had been.

Hell, if I had the money, I'd buy it from her just for the chance to restore it.

But as it was, I was still digging out the hole of debt Dad had left for me to deal with. There was no money —or sense in—imagining things were any different.

Esme stopped in front of the local florist's window, which gave me some time to catch up, but when I was still a few shop fronts away, I slowed. Some guy walked up to her and started up a conversation.

With her back to me, I could only see the guy smiling and Esme nodding. If he were chatting her up, I wasn't about to interrupt. But I wasn't above getting close enough to listen to their conversation.

"So why don't you give me your number?" the guy said.

Damn. He was going for it. Couldn't fault a guy for that.

"Oh. Thanks. But I… don't do that," Esme said politely.

The guy laughed and looked around as if he'd never been shot down before. Then he moved closer to her.

Even with her back to me, I could see her tense. She pulled her purse closer and gripped her shopping bag until her fingers turned white.

That's when I decided it was time to intervene.

I walked up to them just in time to catch the guy's parting words.

"You don't have to be such a bitch about it. You're not all that, anyway," he spat.

Esme's eyes widened at his vitriol, and she stepped back so quickly, she stumbled.

But I was there to keep her upright. And straighten out the asshole who was bothering her.

"Buddy, I think the lady told you to take a hike. But before you do, if you want to keep your front teeth, you'll apologize for calling her a name."

He wrinkled his face and looked me up and down. "Fuck off man. Who the hell do you think you are?"

Esme moved closer to me.

"I'm a guy who doesn't like to see losers like you harassing women. So before you take off, you will say you're sorry. And you'll swear never to talk to another woman like that again."

He turned to walk away.

Big mistake.

I grabbed his upper arm. "Did you hear what I just said?" I growled.

His eyes grew wide, and he tried to wrestle out of my grip. But when he realized that wasn't going to happen, he rolled his eyes.

"Okay. Okay. I'm sorry. I won't do it again."

"Look at her when you say it."

He finally did, and when I released his arm, he took off about as fast as I'd ever seen a scared guy walk.

"Oh my god. What a creep. He was so aggro," Esme said, her face pale.

"Are you okay?"

She nodded. "Yeah. Thank you."

"Hey, do you want to get a coffee?"

She glanced at her watch. "Um. Okay. I could do that. I have twenty minutes before I have to be back at work."

Jesus, don't sound so fucking excited.

We settled into a saggy old sofa in the corner coffee shop.

"What's that you're reading?" she asked, peering into my backpack when I opened it to put my earpods away.

I pulled out my copy of *Infinite Jest* and passed it to her. "It's for my English lit class."

Her eyes widened. "You're in school, that's right."

"Yeah. I had one year left when my dad died. I had to drop out. So now I just take one class at a time. I'll finish one day," I laughed, shaking my head.

Talk about taking the long road.

She flipped through the book. "Why'd you drop out? Was it a money thing?"

"Sort of. There was no one else to run my dad's business. So I had to."

"Wow. That's a big sacrifice."

Seriously. I could have elaborated on how I'd never had any interest in the construction business, and really still didn't, but it didn't seem like the sort of thing to share with a client. Or the fact that the business had been almost belly-up when I took over the reins.

"Dad loved his company, so I wanted to keep it alive. But running it is not a forever thing for me. It's kind of... a temporary arrangement."

That's what I kept telling myself. But the more time that slipped by, the less temporary it seemed.

She shook the hefty book. "I've never read *Infinite Jest*. I've heard it's pretty dense," she said.

I agreed. "I'm slogging through it and am already behind. I have to write a paper on it. And... I have about four weeks to get it all done."

Esme leaned back into her corner of the sofa and studied me. "I'll tell you what. I've always wanted to read this. I'll pick up a copy and we'll read it together."

I laughed. "Are you sure? It's a long-ass book."

She rubbed her chin as she thought. "Yeah. I'm sure. I need something to take my mind off all the... stuff going on in my life. This could be just the thing. I'll even read your paper for you."

She picked up her phone and began tapping.

"What are you doing?" I laughed.

She dropped her phone back into her bag. "There we go. I just ordered it."

I shook my head. "Okay. If that's how you want to spend your free time."

Fuck, she was cute. And now we were going to have our own private little book club. I was down with that. Absolutely.

And it couldn't hurt to have a journalist look over my paper.

The previous coolness I'd seen in her eyes whenever I was around was somehow lessened. In fact, while I could be flattering myself, I could swear it was completely gone.

I couldn't resist her grin any longer. I grabbed one of her hands and pulled her closer to me.

And of course, kissed her.

16

ESME

"Oh my god. The time. Shit, I have to get back to work."

I jumped off the sofa where Case and I had been getting cozy—maybe too cozy—and grabbed my bag.

He stood, too. Close enough to kiss me again.

He still had no idea who I was—the girl he'd kissed under the bleachers senior year of high school. And while the humiliation of that was still fresh for me, I had to say I was pretty damn grateful he didn't remember any of it. It was nice to start with a clean slate.

I'd planned to remind him at some point of our ill-advised liaison of way back when—not to be a pain in the ass, especially since he was being so kind about my house and all. But I was itching to make him squirm at least a little to get a taste of what I had when it all went down.

But I was re-thinking that. Maybe just keep my petty bitterness to myself.

Even better. Let it the fuck go. Completely.

Was I that big of a person?

Probably not.

But as long as he thought I was a happening chick who worked as a journalist at a cool weekly paper, who just so happened to buy a shithole of a house, who was I to change that?

I could see it now. *Remember me from high school when I was awkward and wore thick eyeglasses and you kissed me under the bleachers and then everyone in the school talked like I was a slut?*

Yeah, no. Why bring that shit up?

Not to mention that he'd been my first kiss?

And how all these years later the touch of his lips on mine caused flutters all through my stomach, and if I weren't mistaken, a little wetness *down there*...

I had to get back to work.

"Thank you for the coffee, Case. I'll see you at the house this afternoon, right?"

He stared at me with those damn intense eyes. If I didn't hurry out of there...

"We'll see you later, Esme."

I didn't want to leave. Shit.

"Thank you for the coffee. And for rescuing me."

I wanted to add, thank you also for working on my house. But first things first.

Just before I ran off, he popped a kiss on my cheek.

I hustled the couple blocks back to my office.

I was screwed. Getting cozy with the guys from McKinney Construction? Probably not the best thing to do.

But on the other hand, fuck it. I deserved to have a little fun. Besides, we were only in each other's lives temporarily. They'd be done with their work sooner or later, and I'd be rid of that house.

Maybe I'd even move to a new city. Experience something new.

Nah. Scratch that. I wasn't going anywhere.

"Hey, Esme, do you have a sec?"

I was just getting settled into my cube when Adam appeared.

Dammit. I was so busted for being late. I braced myself for a scolding while I followed him to his office.

I was still trying to catch my breath from having run back to work. Adam always seemed to know when you were the most flustered.

That's when he liked to pounce.

"Es, how are things?" he asked with his smarmy smile.

No. He didn't get to call me by a nickname.

But I beamed, like everything was right in the world. "Great. Just great. How's things by you?"

He ignored my question. "Say, are you still working through the whole emotional upheaval of the left-at-the-altar thing?"

*What?*

Was he fucking kidding?

"Um, why?" I asked slowly, to keep my voice from getting shrill.

He gave me one of those *no big deal* shrugs. "Oh, you know, I was just wondering—"

He could take his wondering and shove it up his ass.

I cut him off, irritation getting the better of me. "That's… not really your business, Adam."

His mouth twitched, but quickly became a smug smile. "Esme. You don't have to get defensive. I mean, c'mon. You're not the first person in the world to get stood up at your wedding," he scoffed.

If I weren't mistaken, he was getting pleasure out of repeating what I'd been through.

*Dick.*

And as if he hadn't already insulted me enough for one day, the fucker doubled down. "I was just wondering because I thought we could, you know, hang out sometime."

And there we had it.

He'd hinted around before about our 'getting to

know each other better,' but just as friends, he'd insisted.

I'd been suspicious he might be interested in more but always just laughed it off.

But no more. "Adam, I'm not comfortable with that." I used my best *let 'em down easy* voice.

It didn't go over very well.

"You know, Esme. Maybe you shouldn't be so *picky*."

Oh no he didn't.

Not only was I going to document this entire goddamn miserable conversation, but I was also tempted to rub right into his face the fact that in the last week I'd been kissed by three of the most gorgeous fucking men I'd ever laid eyes on.

Who also happened to be helping me fix up the house that mister-left-me-at-the-altar had abandoned me with.

He shrugged. "Well, you know, I was thinking you probably didn't have many other options and would be grateful—"

Had he really just used the word *grateful*?

I walked out of his office and when I was back in my cube, Matt shot a glance my way to warn me to stop slamming things around. I ignored him.

Here was this jerk-off of an editor at a free weekly newspaper who acted like the paper under his tutelage was going to become something worthy of a Woodward and Bernstein story, who actually couldn't write his own way out of a paper bag. Seriously. If one of the staff didn't edit his stuff before he let the higher-ups see it, he'd be out on the street faster than he'd gotten fired from the *New York Times*.

His insulting me insulted Case, Alden, and Ty, who were ten times the men Adam was. While I hadn't known them for long, I was massively impressed with how Case had taken over his family business, Alden had stepped up to the plate as a single dad, and Ty was living with the grief of losing his sister.

Everyone had a story, right?

When I thought about it, my little bump in the road —getting stood up at the altar—was something I'd probably laugh about some day. It wasn't the worst thing that could happen to a person.

And it wouldn't define me. No fucking way.

Unlike Adam's relentless efforts to show the *Times* they'd made a mistake in letting him go.

"Esme, one more thing."

Jesus, he was back.

But I smiled. "Yes, Adam?"

"I need an update on the retreat."

Oh right. He actually wanted to talk about work.

I grabbed my notes. "Okay, we've got a ropes course team building activity scheduled for day one, dinner later that night on the outdoor patio, and the all-staff meeting the next day."

He grimaced.

Huh?

"Not… sure that's gonna work," he said, shaking his head.

I couldn't think of a single goddamn thing to say. He'd given me full rein—and *now* he wanted to get involved?

"I'm not sure about the ropes course. In fact, I'm not sure about the team building thing at all. I've always thought they were kind of silly. Look, why don't you cancel all that—"

No. No more.

I thrust my notebook at him. "Here. You do it. I have a story to work on. The woman's conference is coming to town, and I'm behind on scheduling my interviews."

I turned back to my computer and began typing furiously. Exactly what I was typing, I wasn't sure. I could barely see through my rage.

## 17

## ESME

"Hey, look who's here," Ty called.

"Esme, good to see you," Alden added.

Jesus. What a breath of fresh air to walk into a place and be greeted by normal human beings.

I plopped onto one of the kitchen chairs, when Case joined the three of us.

Did they each know the others had kissed me? Was that the sort of thing guys who worked for the same company dished about?

Shit, I hoped not.

"Hey," I said, jumping up, "I got beer. Anybody want to join me in one?"

Work gloves and tool belts came off and the three guys grabbed seats at my kitchen table.

"Hell yeah. Hit me up," Case said, pulling up a chair.

"You have a good day, Esme?" Alden asked, taking a long draw on his beer.

I wanted to spill, but thought better of it. I'd already dumped enough of my problems on these guys.

"Oh, you know," I said breezily, "just dealing with an annoying boss."

Alden clicked his beer bottle against mine. "I hear ya. I have the worst fucking boss on the planet." He snickered and pointed at Case.

But Case's eyes crinkled as he just smiled. "Well, maybe I wouldn't have to be such a dick boss if you did your goddamn job."

They burst out laughing.

I loved their banter, and how they busted on each other.

I turned to Ty. "And how do you fit into this happy little family? I never hear you complain."

He raised his eyebrows. "That's because I hate both these fuckers."

He slapped his knee and roared with laughter.

Christ, it felt good to just sit around and cut up. It felt like I hadn't laughed in way too long.

"Oh shit," Alden said, glancing at his watch, "I gotta get home to Rosie. My mom has a bridge game or something."

He gathered his things and ran for the door. "Thanks for the beer, Esme. See everybody tomorrow."

Case got to his feet, as well. "I have the pleasure of meeting with the clients who love to fight."

I grimaced. "Really? Like they fight right in front of you?"

He took a deep breath. "You would not believe it. They disagree over everything and then turn to me to ask my opinion."

Ty laughed. "So you're their highly-paid mediator, then?"

"Hardly. I am the master of exiting when things get really awkward."

God, I thought I had work problems. I'd never considered what it would be like to have fighting clients.

"Why do you work with them, if they're so diffi-cult?" I asked.

He laughed. "I ask myself the same thing every time I have to talk to them. It's a big job that will be good for the company. But I doubt they'll be together for long at the rate they are going."

"Or they could be like my parents—happy in their misery," Ty added.

"Geez. Maybe I'm lucky I grew up with only one parent." I laughed.

Case headed for the door. "See you all tomorrow."

I looked at Ty. "Another beer?"

He smiled and nodded. "Seems like we're the only ones with no responsibility. At the moment, anyway."

"It feels good, doesn't it?" I asked.

He set his beer down. "Hey, there was something I wanted to show you on the front porch. Where I was making some wood repairs. Can I show you?"

"Let's do it."

I followed Ty to the front door, trying not to stare too hard at his butt. I was all warm and toasty from my beer-and-a-half, and the annoyances from earlier in the day were momentarily shelved.

"Okay," he said, crouching and gesturing for me to follow, "this here is dry rot. We can either try to use filler on it, or replace the wood altogether—"

Just then a massive, hairy spider came creeping out of the empty space where the wood was missing. I shrieked, falling back onto my ass. Heart thumping, I scrambled to my feet and ran down the house's front steps to get away from the creature.

Ty got to his feet and watched me, puzzled. "Um. Are you okay Esme?" he asked.

"Did.... did you see that giant... *thing*?" I asked breathlessly.

He nodded. "Yeah, of course. How could I miss it? It's a wolf spider. They're all over the place. When you do the kind of work I do, you run into them all the time."

Oh god. I was going to puke.

"You have to deal with them all the time?"

He walked down the steps toward me and reached for my hand. "C'mon. Let's go back inside. I think you sufficiently scared off the little guy, so it's you who needs to calm down now."

I took a deep breath and let him lead me into the house. Once we were back inside, I leaned against the closed door, still shaking.

Yeah, I had a serious case of arachnophobia.

He stepped closer to me and put a hand on my shoulder. With his other hand, he smoothed a lock of hair behind my ear. "You feeling a little better?" he asked in a quiet voice.

I nodded. "Yeah. I think so. Sorry about the freak out."

"It's okay," he said, his warm breath whispering against my neck. "Just take a couple deep breaths."

To hell with the spider—I had a gorgeous man in front of me who was trying to comfort me.

And other things.

I laid my head back against the door and closed my eyes as Ty's lips brushed over my temple, then down my cheek.

Time stood still. There was nothing else in the world but the two of us. I put my hands on either side of his face and pulled him to me.

"Goddamn, you're sexy," he murmured, pressing his forehead to mine in a deliciously intimate gesture.

"You're not so bad yourself," I teased, taking him by the hand.

He smiled down at me and led me up the stairs to my bedroom. I couldn't believe I was letting him, but at the same time, it was all I could do not to run him over getting to my room.

He set me on the edge of my bed and pulled off my sneakers, then laid me back. His warm hands ran up my thighs until my dress was pushed clear to my panties, and his warm breath hovered outside them.

It was torture. Pure torture. I grabbed at the sheets under me for some sort of purchase and pushed my hips up toward him without even thinking about it. I wanted his mouth on me, and I wasn't going to be able to wait long.

Fortunately, he got the message. As he slid the crotch of my panties aside, I shivered from the cool air on my sex and the anticipation of what was to come.

His tongue flicked my pussy lips without parting them, leaving me squirming and grinding.

A moment later, his tongue invaded me, running from my clit to ass and back as he pulled the crotch of my panties well out of the way. A jolt shot up my spine, and I tensed as one and then two of his fingers entered me.

With a 'come here' motion, he tickled me until an orgasm struck. I arched, my body convulsing and my hand slamming the bed under me.

"Oh my god, Ty," I whispered, my thighs trembling on either side of his head.

He moved up between my legs until he could reach my lips to share what he had just tasted. After what felt like an eternity of delicious kisses, his fingers wandered through my tangled hair before he flipped me over on my side and wrapped his arms around me tightly like a nesting spoon.

# 18

## ALDEN

"HOW'S THE LIFE OF THE TOWN'S MOST ELIGIBLE bachelor?"

Case glared like I knew he would. But I was beginning to suspect that deep down, he sort of liked it.

Not so much because it helped him pick up chicks —that wasn't really his thing. Rather, it gave him something to lighten up about.

I was aware of the shape the business was in when Mr. McKinney passed. He hadn't kept it a secret, at least not from me, which I was grateful for. I learned a lot from him about how to run a business.

And how not to run a business.

Case looked over my shoulder to make sure his mother couldn't hear and rolled his eyes. "Dude, it's awesome. Everywhere I go, women are just tearing their clothes off."

I laughed. "For the likes of you? I doubt it."

He shook his head. "You know, I've decided to laugh about it rather than be annoyed. Everyone has their problems, right? Look at Esme. Her fiancé bailed and left her with a money pit of a house. But do you see her walking around with a cloud over her head?"

He was right. Esme had her ups and downs, no doubt, but she wasn't letting the recent shit in her life push her off track. She had work that she liked, friends, and from what I could see, a supportive and devoted dad.

Not too shabby if you asked me.

"Speaking of Esme," I said, "what's this I hear about her helping you with your school work?"

"Oh yeah. She offered to read the paper I'm writing for my English lit class," he said. "Not sure I'll have her do it, but I appreciate her interest, of course."

"Well. Nice. Very nice."

He narrowed his eyes at me. "If I didn't know better, I might say you have a certain amount of interest in our lovely client, too."

Ah-ha.

"*Too*? So you're admitting you're into her? I knew it."

And I didn't blame him one bit.

Or Ty, for that matter.

Esme was a kick-ass chick. There was just no other way to put it.

He nodded. "I do like her. If I didn't, I wouldn't be working on her house. None of us would. It's not like we're in it for the money, that's for damn sure."

I looked around the office that used to be Mr. McKinney's. "I didn't think I'd ever be interested in another woman after Rosie's mom bailed on us. That just seemed too big of a betrayal to move on from. And yet I feel so... peaceful around Esme."

Case took a deep breath. "What are we going to do about this? And what if Ty likes her too? It's not like we can all date her, you know what I mean?"

I thought for a moment. I'd had an idea when I realized I wasn't the only one with the hots for Esme, but wasn't sure if I should bring it up.

Only one way to find out.

"You know, maybe we all *can* date her. We don't know yet where Ty stands on things, but from watching the way he looks at her, I have a feeling he's on the same page we are."

Case nodded. "All of us date her, huh? Interesting idea. Could be hot. Very hot," he said as a smile grew across his face.

I knew he was a wild man at heart. He just hadn't had time lately to let his freak flag fly.

"You ever do anything like that?" he asked.

"Yeah. Back before I met Rosie's mom. It was great. Super hot."

He shrugged. "Oh, who am I kidding? I don't have time for dating or anything like that." He jumped up from behind his desk and closed his door softly.

It must not be easy working with your mother. No damn privacy.

He sat back down. "Dude, as soon as I finish my degree, I want to go for an MBA."

Christ. From the frying pan into the fire.

"What about the company?" I asked, trying to sound as casual as I could.

And for good reason. I'd always hoped Case would make me a partner in the company. His father had mentioned it on more than one occasion and when he died, for a moment, my dream died with him. But Case needed me. McKinney construction needed me.

But I wasn't going to bring it up. Yet. I needed Case to realize he could trust me to run the place when he wasn't around—which sounded like it could be pretty frequently if he had graduate school plans.

It wasn't like I had a ton of extra time to devote to the business myself. But I had my mother ready to help with Rosie any time I needed her. Thank god. The woman was a saint.

Case rose from his seat again. "Shall we head out? It's time to get to the old Buckner place."

I grabbed my backpack and led the way toward one of the company trucks.

"When are you going to stop calling it the Buckner place?" I asked once we were in the truck.

Case thought for a moment. "You're right. I need to stop doing that. What should we call it, then?"

"For as long as she owns it, why don't we call it the new Rutherford place?"

He laughed. "Works for me," he said, pulling into traffic for the short ride to her place.

"Ty, you look seriously tired, my friend."

Our resident woodworker gazed around the room, avoiding our eyes and started measuring a piece of trim.

A piece of trim he'd measured not two minutes earlier.

Case shot me a glance and winked. "Hey, Alden, I think after you and I left last night, Ty might have had… a little fun time with our friend Esme."

No shit.

If we hadn't been suspicious before, Ty had just confirmed everything.

He finally smiled and looked up at us. "Guilty as

charged. But I don't kiss and tell." He put his hands on the tool belt hanging around his waist as if he were daring us to dig for details.

But that's not what we were after.

Case nodded. "It's all good, man. Alden and I were just talking about Esme this morning. Looks like we're all interested."

Ty's eyebrows rose.

I got it. He wasn't sure whether this was good news or bad.

He put his hands up like a *stop* sign. "Guys. I don't mean to tread on anyone's territory. If this is going to be an issue for our working together—or our friendship—just say the word. I'm not going to mess things up for a woman who just got her heart broken and is probably just trying to sow some wild oats anyway."

"Esme's intentions aside, that's not the issue at all, Ty," I said. "We have an idea we wanted to run past you."

His eyebrows rose. "Lay it on me."

"If Esme is down with it, how 'bout we all date her?"

He looked between the two of us before he spoke, like he was trying to assess how serious we were. "That's... quite an idea. I guess we could... bring it up with her. Where do we start?"

Before we could answer, Ty did it for us. "I'll tell you what. How 'bout everyone come over to my place tonight for dinner? It'll probably just be take-out but I feel like celebrating."

Case frowned. "It might be a little too early to start celebrating—"

But Ty cut him off. "I didn't mean celebrating about Esme, although you never know. I have something else to celebrate."

After a pause, he broke into a huge smile. "It's not that big of a deal, really, but I'm pretty fucking happy about it. A chair I designed just won a national award."

Case crossed the room in three long steps and held his hand out in congratulations, slapping Ty on the back with his other hand. "No shit. Brother, that's killer news."

I did the same. "Wow, Ty. Congrats, man."

Ty was all kinds of talented with wood, and I'd wondered on more than one occasion if his fixing up dry rot on old buildings was just a way to pay the bills on the way to something bigger. Looked like he might be on his way.

He scrolled through his phone and showed us the chair, a sleek mid-century design with incredibly beautifully turned wood.

"Jesus, dude. Sign me up. I'm buying one," I said.

I should have asked first how much it was, but I would do anything to support my friend.

"Shit," Case laughed, "I'll take *two*."

I had a feeling Esme was going to be quite happy for Ty as well.

"All right. I'll tell Esme about dinner, and we'll meet at my place at seven," he said.

Case rubbed his beard. "What if she's busy?"

Ty just smiled as he picked up a sledgehammer. "I'll tell her to cancel her plans."

I liked how that man took care of business.

19

———————

ALDEN

"YOUR PLACE IS AMAZING, TY," ESME SAID, TAKING IN the ranch house he'd lovingly restored. "And look at this."

She shook her head at the nearly-all glass wall on the back of his house, which overlooked a swimming pool and empty land for as far as the eye could see.

Esme was about to learn a lot about Ty.

He handed us all a beer and raised his bottle. "Here's to… a lot of stuff."

Puzzled, Esme looked at us as we laughed. "Is there something going on I don't know about? Did you guys burn my house down today? Or find a million dollars hidden in the walls? Because if I had the choice, I think I would take the money."

I was pretty sure she wouldn't mind too much if the place burned to the ground, but I understood about the appeal of the money.

My little Rosie, snuggled into the baby carrier on my chest, stirred in her sleep, smacking her milk-covered lips.

"First of all," Ty said, "we have baby Rosie with us tonight." He walked over and slipped a finger into her tiny little fist, and she reflexively grabbed him back.

"Then, we have our favorite client, Esme."

She looked around the room and blushed a little. God, she was cute.

"And… we're celebrating my national recognition." He led us to his den, where the work of art sat in a corner.

"Dude, that should be in the middle of the room, not in a corner. It's freaking amazing," Case said, running his fingers over the smooth, dark wood.

"Wait. This chair won an award? Did you make this?" Esme asked with wide eyes, smoothing her hand over the back rail.

Ty nodded with pride. "I did. It's walnut, my favorite wood. I'm going to build a whole collection around it."

"Holy shit, congrats," Esme cried, throwing her arms around him.

Case and I looked at each other. Of course.

Ty embraced Esme right back, not releasing her as quickly as if it were just a casual hug.

"Can I sit in it?" she asked, bouncing up and down.

"Be my guest."

She sat down, carefully at first, as if the chair were fragile. Then she swiveled around on the smooth wood and leaned back. "Oh my god. It's heavenly."

I took a seat in a crackly old leather club chair, running my hand over Rosie's hair, and Case and Ty settled into his overstuffed sofa.

"Your parents must be so proud of you," she said.

That's when Ty's face took on a pained expression. "Eh. It's not really their thing."

Puzzled, Esme wrinkled her nose. "How could they not be excited?"

Ty might have spent some intimate time with Esme, but he sure hadn't told her much about his family. I didn't blame him.

"Well, I told you my sister died, right?" he asked.

She nodded slowly.

"My parents blame me for it. So I don't have much of a relationship with them. And my work... further alienated them."

"Oh. Shit," she said quietly.

He nodded.

Way to put a damper on the party. But what the

hell. She had to know if she was going to… hang out with us guys.

So I decided to help. "Ty is from the Wells family."

Esme shot me a blank look. "Okay. So?"

She clearly wasn't familiar with the world of commercial real estate. Which was to be expected. I'd never paid any attention to it until I'd met Ty.

"My family is… shall we say, pretty well off. Before my sister died, I'd been following my dream of working with wood like this, rather than going into the family business or becoming a doctor or lawyer. Then when she passed, they pretty much cut me off," he said.

"How did you get this amazing house?" Esme asked.

Okay. Now, she was getting it.

"I have—well, *had*—a trust from my grandfather. I'd always used my money pretty wisely. Not so much my sister."

Shit. He was going there. He didn't share this part of his story very readily.

He looked down at his hands. "She… was into drugs and stuff. I was out with her the night she OD'd. My father blames me."

Esme's hand flew to her mouth. "Oh my god. That's terrible."

He nodded. "We'd gone to a concert with a bunch of her friends. She'd sworn to me she wasn't using, but… well, she passed out and by the time I got her to the hospital… she was gone."

Ty cleared his throat and stretched his neck as if he could chase the bad memories away.

But we all knew that was impossible.

He forced a small smile. "So that's why they're not too interested in that little chair you're sitting in winning an award."

The doorbell rang. Thank god. The air in the room was thick with tragedy. And regret.

"Chinese food is here," he said, jumping to his feet.

Esme stood and took his hand. They headed to the front door, leaning into each other.

Ty might have been through some shit, but I wagered to say things were starting to look up for the man.

## 20

ESME

"DAMN, GIRL. I CAN OFFICIALLY SAY, I AM JEALOUS OF you."

Words I never thought I'd hear come out of Charli's mouth.

I pulled my car into the parking lot at work. "Hey Char, gotta go. I'm late for work as it is. Talk to you later," I said, swiping my phone closed.

How was I going to focus today? My head was spinning.

The previous night, with all the guys and me over at Ty's for dinner, was… unexpected to say the least.

I couldn't stop replaying every last detail.

First, Ty lived in one of the most fucking awesome houses I'd ever seen.

Then, I found out he came from a loaded family, who, unfortunately, had pretty much cast him out. Their loss. He was such a special guy.

Next, the guys wanted to date me. Like, all of them. At once. Together and shit. Which was about the weirdest fucking thing I'd ever heard.

One of the hottest, too.

And last, well, let's just say I'd never been around so much male beauty.

After we'd stuffed our faces with killer Chinese food, we migrated to Ty's back deck, where he had a pool and hot tub and views to die for. Jasmine bushes scented the air, and string lights cast a romantic, bistro-type glow.

I felt like a kid in a candy store. Beautiful setting with three freaking gorgeous men. I couldn't think of anything else in the world I wanted.

And that was only the beginning.

It was a lovely night—perfect, really—and it was just beginning to heat up.

It started after Alden put little Rosie down in Ty's guest room. He joined us on the deck, alternatively stretching and touching his toes.

"I love carrying around my little girl, but you can only do that for so long," he said, his body making several cracking sounds.

Case sat back in his chair, sipping the scotch Ty had just poured him. "Why don't you take a swim, Alden? The pool's heated."

Kicking his own shoes off, Case pulled his T-shirt over his

Alden stood for a moment, staring at the water, which was glittering under the swaying lights. "Yeah. I think I will."

And just like that, he dropped his pants, pulled his shirt over his head, and dove in.

But not before taking off his boxer shorts, too.

*Okay.*

I was getting the picture.

Ty got up from his lounge chair and pulled off the elastic holding his man bun. In seconds, his clothes were off, too.

Holy crap. I'd felt lucky enough sitting around with these gorgeous men. And now they were disrobing in front of me?

While Alden swam the length of the pool under water, Ty walked around to the far side of it, his hard ass flexing with every step. He climbed up on the diving board, and when he got to the end of it, bounced up and down before he, too, dove in.

But not before I got a good look at his lovely cock.

"Why don't you take a picture? Lasts longer," Case teased, catching me staring.

Alden and Ty hollered, each trying to splash the other with a bigger wall of water.

I turned toward Case. "Aren't you going in, too?"

He leaned forward, cupping my chin. "I don't know. Will you go in?"

Oh god. The way this man touched me was dangerous. Even though I'd been with Ty only the night before, with the warm evening breeze and delicious scotch, I was dying to just straddle Case and brush my lips all over his muscular chest.

But I didn't get the chance to do that because he shot to his feet, dropped his jeans, and cannonballed into the pool inches away from the other guys.

Incredible. Was this my life taking a turn for the better? Only a month earlier, I'd been stuffed into the wedding dress from hell that I'd let Charli's mom talk me into, ready to marry someone because I thought it was *the thing to do*, only to be stood up at the altar in front of two hundred people, most of whom I didn't even know.

And now I was watching three hunky construction guys splash around naked in a pool at one of the most bitching houses I'd ever seen.

Was someone playing a trick on me? Because I couldn't possibly deserve this. I was a struggling journalist at a free weekly where I was paid terribly, with an albatross of a house around my neck that should probably have been burned to the ground long ago.

But shit, I might as well enjoy the moment.

I got to my feet, pulled my dress over my head, threw my bra and panties aside, and dove into the pool, too.

When I came up for air, I paddled to the edge and leaned against it to enjoy the starry night and my handsome friends.

Making sure all my bits were well beneath the surface of the water.

"Look at that pretty girl over there," Case called.

"Don't be shy, buddy," Ty teased, "go see if she'll talk to you."

Stifling my laughter, I looked aside and pretended to ignore them.

But that was not possible when Case swam over and put his arms on either side of me, effectively pinning me between himself and the edge of the pool.

High school was suddenly a hundred years ago, forgotten and unimportant.

Thank god.

"Well, hello," he said.

I tilted my head. "Do I *know* you?" I asked dramatically.

He shook his head, staring intently at me in the twinkling light. "No. But you'll want to."

"Oh, really?" I demanded.

"Yup. After you see the way I kiss you," he breathed.

His lips found mine, soft and exploring at first, then

hard and bruising. I closed my eyes as his hands held my face, then drifted down my shoulders to my back. They stopped on my ass, which he kneaded in his callused hands.

Startled, I heard a low whistle come from across the pool. I'd almost forgotten Ty and Alden were there.

"Whew, look at those two," Ty called.

Case stopped kissing me long enough to turn around. "Why don't you come over here and join us?"

Oh my god. Did he really say that?

Alden swam under the water toward me and bobbed up right next to us, turning my face toward his while Case kept playing with my behind.

Alden's kiss was different—more patient somehow, but equally delicious. He grabbed a hank of my wet hair and tilted my head back to run his lips over my neck.

Wow.

That's when I felt Case's fingers find the slick folds between my thighs, which he stroked until he found my clit. With his thumb, he made small circles until I gasped from the sensation. His hard cock bounced against my leg, so I reached for it with one hand and found Alden's with my other.

Holy shit. I was holding two cocks.

The pool water swayed, and I opened my eyes to see Ty boost himself up to sit on the edge of the pool, right next to us.

"Hey, beautiful," he said, leaning down to kiss my forehead. I just wanted a better view."

"I've got an idea," Alden said. "Esme, sit up on the edge of the pool."

I climbed out, my skin springing alive with goose-bumps, my nipples growing pointy in reaction to the night breeze.

"Now scoot down until you're on the very edge," he said.

Oh. Okay. *Now* I got it.

As soon as my butt was hanging over the edge, Alden pushed my knees up.

"Can you help me, boys?" he asked.

What the hell?

Ty took a hold of one of my knees, and Case the other, and between the two of them, I was spread wide open for all of them to see.

And I loved it.

Alden whistled quietly. "Look at this beautiful pussy, boys. So pink and shiny."

My sex clenched as Alden, still in the pool, lowered his mouth to my slit, running up and down until he settled on my clit. His lips first waved over my hard nub, and then his tongue circled it until I was convulsing and greedy with unrelenting need.

He set one finger at my opening and gently entered me, followed by another finger, his pumping matching the sucking on my clit. The guys gripped my thighs and pulled them as far apart as they would go as I began to thrash, my entire body convulsing with an almost unbearable orgasm.

I dropped my head back, and the air swirled around me as I came again, oblivious to anyone or anything except my throbbing pussy.

"Oh god, Alden," I whispered.

"Guys, let's get her up and to that chair over there," Case said.

Alden jumped out of the water and followed as Case and Ty helped me to a lounge chair.

"How are you feeling baby?" Case asked as I lay back.

"Mmmm, good," I murmured.

He ran the back of his fingers over one of my breasts, sending a jolt of sensation right back down to my core. "You want some more?"

I nodded weakly. "Yes, please."

"Okay. Get on your knees."

I looked up at him and extended a hand for help. I flipped over onto my knees, the lounge cushion flexing beneath me, and heard a rustle of plastic.

Ah. The condom.

"Head down," Case growled, positioning himself behind me.

With my legs open and my head down, my ass was pretty much up in the air for all to see. I wagged my backside around so everyone could get a good look, and when I felt Case at my opening, I pushed back. That was how eager I was to have him inside me.

He reached forward and grabbed one of my breasts. "You ready, baby?" he asked.

I lifted my head slightly. "Yeah. Please."

He slowly pushed inside until I was stretched to my limit. And still I wanted more, so I pushed back until his balls slapped against my clit. I turned my head sideways and saw Alden sitting on a lounge chair smiling, and Ty standing, stroking the erection in his hand.

Case's pumping picked up speed until he was driving me so hard I had to hold the shaking chair frame below me. Orgasm after orgasm washed over me until I lost track of, well, everything.

Finally, he bellowed behind me, burying himself one last time to empty his load. His cock pulsed as he came, his voice raspy and raw.

When he pulled out, I was lucky Ty was there to catch me. He helped me to my feet and to his bedroom, where he brought me to the shower. We stood under a thick stream of warm water as he soaped my body and massaged delicious-smelling shampoo through my hair.

A guy who could wash hair? Had I landed on a different planet?

When we finished, he gently towel-dried my body and then my hair with thick plushy towels, pulled a T-shirt over my head, and led me to his bed.

I suppose at some point Case and Alden had left to go home because when I woke up the next morning, I was alone. But I was also happy, satisfied, and maybe a little bit sore.

CHARLI, the good BFF that she was, continued to text me all day at work, telling me what a lucky bitch I was to have had not just a threesome, but a foursome, something even *she* had never done.

I'd graduated to a new level of sexual respect in her eyes.

Life goals, and all that.

"Yo, Esme," Matt called over our cube wall, "you coming to happy hour Friday?"

Oh. Shit. With all the planning, or should I say un-planning, of the retreat, I'd forgotten about *City Scene's* monthly happy hour.

"Yeah. I guess."

I also remembered that Charli had invited me to a wine and cheese at her mom's boutique the same night. I'd have to juggle both.

Which I was sure I could do.

After all, I'd just juggled three men and was feeling pretty freaking badass.

## 21

TY

I PICKED UP MY BIGGEST SLEDGEHAMMER AND BROUGHT it down again and again on the old wood cabinets in Esme's kitchen.

It felt good.

I was taking a chance, I knew. We'd not discussed working on her kitchen, but the cabinets were just so old and beat up that I figured I'd rebuild them as a surprise. While we didn't have the time or budget to completely redo the kitchen, this much of a facelift would go a long way when she went to resell.

As the brittle wood splintered, I thought back to the night before and how confidently our beautiful girl had handled us three guys. She was hot as shit, no doubt about it, and the way she responded to our touch was sexy as fuck.

And now, even though I was swinging a freaking sledgehammer, I was getting a hard-on thinking about her.

"Damn, buddy. You're destroying the place," Alden said, poking his head into the kitchen to see what all the noise was.

I stopped to wipe the sweat off my face. "Yeah, well, gotta get these piece of shit cabinets out of the way."

"Seriously? You're putting new ones in? I didn't know that was part of the job."

I was glad I'd started the demolition before either Case or Alden stopped me. And now that half the cabinets were nothing more than splinters of wood, there was no turning back.

"It… wasn't. But it is now," I said matter-of-factly.

He nodded. "So how'd it go last night after we left?"

"I put her to bed, and she was still snoozing when I left this morning."

I knew that if I woke her up before I left, I'd never get out of the house.

"You think she liked our proposition?" he asked.

I had to think about that one. "Hard to tell. I mean, we all had a freaking hot time, that's for sure. But who knows whether she wants to… take it further."

I hoped like hell she did. I know all us guys did. A

woman like Esme didn't come along every day. Actually, a woman like Esme never came along, if you asked me. It used to be that all I dated were girls from my private school, and then later, my parents' club. And I'd never been more miserable.

When I was finally out from under their thumb, I mostly just hooked up with girls I met in bars. Not to pat myself on the back, but it seemed there was no shortage of women wanting to hook up with a decent-looking guy.

And for the time being, that suited me fine. Since I'd lost my sister, I'd not had it in me to do anything more than one-nighters. I still had nightmares about the night she OD'd. On one hand, I hoped I always would. I didn't want to forget. And I supposed, wanted to keep punishing myself, too.

My parents were certainly doing that successfully.

But all that was background noise now.

Something about Esme clicked for me, like it did for the other guys. She was a determined journalist, and while she might not be working for a big and prestigious publication, she was following her dream.

Like I was.

Case woke me out of my reverie. "Hey, it's six o'clock. I'm heading out. See you tomorrow?"

"Of course. Going to meet up with Esme in a bit. She invited me to her work happy hour or something."

Case gave me the thumbs up. "Have a great time and say hello to our girl."

*Our* girl. Yeah, she was totally our girl. Even if she didn't know it yet.

He winked at me and left.

I ran upstairs and into Esme's shower to clean up.

## TY

I SPOTTED HER FROM ACROSS THE BAR, TALKING AND laughing with her coworkers, just like the first time I'd seen her.

And not been able to take my eyes off her.

She was beautiful with her porcelain skin and long dark hair, but what drew me the most was her quiet, sexy, no-nonsense approach to life. She might have had some setbacks like everybody does, but she didn't dwell on them.

She was left at the altar holding the bag on a practically worthless house, and without blinking, got to work having it fixed up for sale. She didn't sit around feeling sorry for herself. I just don't think she had the time. Or patience.

"Ty! Over here!" she called, waving over all the heads.

And as I entered the circle of her work people, I noticed I was getting a lot of stares. I didn't blame anyone. They knew what she'd fairly recently been through, and probably wondered who the hell the new guy was.

I'd be thinking the same way.

"Hey, gorgeous," I said, bending to kiss her cheek.

A couple of her colleagues' eyes widened, as I knew they would.

"Everybody, this is my friend Ty Wells." She introduced me around, ending with a scrawny guy with glasses and highlighted hair named Adam.

*This* was her boss?

After watching us for a few minutes and waiting until we had beers in hand, he cornered us.

"Esme," he said in an oily voice, his hand on my arm, "you didn't tell me you were friends with Ty Wells."

She shrugged. "Do you guys know each other or something?"

Adam gazed up at me, ignoring her question. "Well, you know, the Wells are a very special family."

Oh. I got it. He was one of *those*.

Esme laughed politely. "Of course he comes from a special family. He's pretty special himself."

Nice.

Adam waved a dismissive hand at her. "Esme—" he started to say in the most condescending tone ever.

She had to work every day with this little fucker?

"—the Wells family is the biggest commercial real estate developer in the state. Haven't you ever seen the huge signs on office buildings that say Wells Development?"

She looked at me and back at him. He didn't seem to understand not everyone was impressed by family name and money.

"Yeah. I've seen them."

He rolled his eyes. "And you know what that means?"

Enough.

"Why don't you tell us what that means to you, Adam? Because you seem pretty excited to talk about my family and me, which is interesting, considering I'm standing right here."

His head snapped back with indignation. I hated little fuckers like that, and I hated even more that he got to breathe the same air as Esme. Or anyone else, for that matter.

But he recovered quickly. People like that always did.

He smiled and laughed nervously. "Okay, okay.

Look, Ty, I didn't mean to make anyone uncomfortable."

His hand was back on my arm. "Say, both of you. I have some friends"—he looked around and lowered his voice— "who are very influential people in town."

He looked at us like he was sharing gold.

"There is a party this coming weekend. I'd be happy to bring you as my guests."

Was he for real? Did he really think we wanted to spend a second more with him than we had to, not to mention his *influential people*?

I took a swig of my beer and stuffed my empty hand in my pocket to fight the temptation to wipe the smug right off his face.

Esme moved closer to me to deliver a discreet nudge. "Oh wow. Thank you so much, Adam. I love meeting *influential people*. But would you have invited me to this if I weren't a friend of Ty's? Because I don't remember you ever inviting me to anything before."

His face got long as the fake-ass smile slithered from it and his lips pressed into a thin line.

"Well... I... never thought you'd be interested, Esme," he lied.

Whatever, dude.

And once again, he recovered quickly, like the Terminator sprouting new body parts every time he needed them. "Look. If you guys ever change your mind, just let me know. You know where to find me."

He squeezed my arm for emphasis and wandered off.

Esme looked down for a moment, then took a deep breath. "I'm so sorry," she whispered.

I threw an arm around her shoulder. "Eh. It happens. No need to be embarrassed. I'm not. Hey, you wanna get out of here?"

She nodded. "Yeah. Let's do it. I'm just going to run to the ladies' room."

It wasn't until we were in my truck that I realized how pale Esme was. So I reached for her hand.

"Look, Esme. Shit like that happens to me all the time. I thought most assholes like your boss would be a little more discreet about their intentions, but I guess there are always exceptions. Christ, that guy was a piece of work."

She nodded. "He's awful. Just awful. I feel so badly you had to be humiliated that way."

"I've been dealing with this all my life. I feel badly that *you* had to be humiliated by that little weasel."

I pulled up in front of her house, but I could tell neither of us was ready to say goodnight.

"Coming in?" she asked with a sly smile.

Shit. I didn't need to be asked twice.

We walked up to her house hand in hand. It felt good. I didn't hold hands with my one-nighters. It was just too intimate, and besides, I didn't want to give them the wrong idea.

"I'd offer you something, but my kitchen is under construction," she joked.

"Speaking of which, come see what I got done today."

I led her to the kitchen and watched her eyes widen.

"Oh my god. *This* is what custom cabinets look like?"

She stepped over my building mess, and smoothed a hand along one of the finished cabinet doors. "I don't think I've ever seen anything so beautiful. This is amazing. Actually, this is going to make the rest of the house look more shabby than it already is."

I laughed. "Don't worry. With a new coat of paint, everything will look fine."

She looked up at me. "I want to pay you for this. I'm not sure how I will, but I'll find a way."

And that's what I loved about this girl.

She didn't take things for granted or live like the world owed her anything. So different from the women I met from my parents' club.

"Let's go upstairs," I said.

I undressed her slowly, wanting to savor every bit of her smooth skin. When she was naked, I spun her slowly so I could take her in.

She left me breathless.

"You're so beautiful," I said as I laid her back on the bed.

She pulled the elastic out of my hair and ruffled her

hands through the tangled mess. "What do your parents think of your long hair?"

Lying next to her, I ran my fingers along her stomach. "They don't much like it. But then, they don't much like anything about me."

She propped herself up on her elbow. "How can that be? I mean, you're a good guy. Just because you didn't fit into their mold, they felt they could discard you?"

As much as it hurt to hear that, it was a good way to describe the situation.

"It's more my dad than my mom. She pretty much just follows him. But he's got a giant ego, and anyone who doesn't do what he wants, he takes as a giant insult against him."

"Um, I think that's called a narcissist."

I flopped onto my back. "It was actually kind of funny. He wanted me to become a doctor so badly, and I can't stand the sight of blood. It was never a remote possibility, and yet he still hounds me. Calls me a *bohemian.*"

She laughed. "I guess he means that as an insult. But I'd take it as a compliment."

I returned my attention to her. I wasn't willing to get sidetracked talking about my crazy family. There were much more pressing matters at hand.

I peeled off my T-shirt and got between my girl's

legs. I'd enjoyed her the night before, no doubt, but to have her to myself for a bit was a pure delight.

I ran kisses up her inner thighs as she welcomed me with open legs, scraping her nails on my scalp as I got closer to her sex.

"Such a pretty pussy," I murmured before I ran my tongue between her swollen lips.

"Oh god," she whispered, "that feels so nice. But, Ty?"

I looked up. "Yes, baby?"

She gave me that damn dazzling smile. "I think I need you inside me."

I laughed. "I suppose I could help with that."

Before discarding the rest of my clothes, I pulled a condom from my pocket and sheathed myself.

"Ty?"

I crawled back to my position between her lovely legs. "Yeah?" I asked, dropping light kisses on her breasts.

"Does it bother you that I was with the other guys last night?"

Ah. That. It was bound to come up.

"I'm good with it, baby. We discussed it, and actually… we find it kind of hot. So don't worry about being judged. That's bullshit."

She beamed and pulled closer.

I entered her slowly, and when she dropped her

head back and closed her eyes with a sigh, I picked up the pace.

I wasn't going to last long, but wanted to make sure she was taken care of first.

As I slipped in and out of her warm folds, she began to shudder. Then she dug her nails into my ass and pulled me all the way in with a scream.

"Oh god, Ty, fuck me," she cried.

Well, that was all it took. Her pussy contracted around my tortured cock, and we came together, our foreheads touching, feeling each other's breath.

We collapsed but held each other, and as we caught our breath, I spied the jewelry box with the spinning ballerina, like the one my sister used to have.

And something about it didn't bother me as much anymore.

## ESME

"Well, it was nice to meet your boyfriend the other night. Didn't take you long, did it?"

Did he *really* just say that?

Wait a minute. This was Adam, my asshole boss. Of course he just said that.

He was the champion of finding a sore spot and twisting a knife in it. If they gave rewards for thoughtless cruelty, he'd surely win.

"First, Ty is not my boyfriend. And second, even if he were, it's none of your business."

Probably wasn't smart to be such a bitch to him, but he needed to back the fuck off.

He sat one of his butt cheeks on the corner of my desk. "Oh c'mon, Esme. Lighten up. We're one big happy family here. You know that."

Now that he was so close, I could smell whatever crap it was he put in his hair.

He opened his hands. "I figured he was your new guy and that's why you shut me down."

Was he so clueless he completely missed my disdain for him? What a way to go through life. Must be nice to be so immune to reality.

"Ty is working on my house. He's an expert wood-worker. In fact, a chair he designed just won an award."

Adam was unimpressed. "That's nice," he said dismissively. "I can't believe you didn't know who he was. His family is richer than god. And he's much better looking than that guy who stood you up at the altar."

"Adam, I have some work I need to get done, not to mention trying to resurrect that staff retreat—"

He put a hand on my arm. "Look, Esme, I am here to talk to you about work. Take a chill pill."

*Chill pill?* Did people still say that? Besides, everyone knew that telling someone to 'take a chill pill' always had the opposite effect.

How long would I go to prison if I stabbed Adam with my just-sharpened pencil?

"Okay. What's up?" I asked as sweetly as I could.

"I have an idea for an assignment for you."

Okay. Now we're talking.

"That's great. I hope it doesn't have to do with planning another event," I said, joking-not-joking.

"No, don't be silly. I want you to do a story."

He had me by the balls—so to speak. He knew I was always looking to prove my journalistic chops and that I was forever gunning for more and better story assignments.

"Okay. What's it about? What's the angle?"

I tried to tone down the excitement in my voice. Not sure it worked.

He tapped his chin like he'd just had the idea of a lifetime. I braced myself.

"Why don't you… do a story on Ty Wells?" he said in a perky voice.

My short-lived excitement oozed away like the last bit of air in a leaky balloon.

"Um, Ty? As in my friend Ty?" I stumbled.

I so wanted him to tell me I'd misheard him. I really, really wanted to believe there was something redeeming about my boss, that he was not completely unprincipled, and that he'd never throw me into the sort of conflict of interest that could end a journalist's career.

Right.

He smiled like he'd won the lottery. "Yeah. Ty Wells."

My mouth flapped open and closed a few times

while I found my words. "Um, Adam, I'm not sure I'm comfortable—"

He waved his hand like he was shooing a fly. "Nonsense. Good journalism isn't about being comfortable. Back when I was at the *New York Times*..."

While he droned on about his entry level job at the *Times* like he'd been the freaking editor-in-chief there, all the reasons it would be wrong for me to do a story on Ty scrolled through my mind like they were on repeat.

And they all ended with *no fucking way*.

I WAS on my way to the local steak place to meet the guys for dinner while Adam's request haunted me. I'd had such a busy day between planning our stupid work retreat and getting ready for my women's conference interviews that I'd not had time to ruminate on his audacious proposal.

Now that I did, I was getting pissed.

Had there ever been anyone so fucking clueless?

And as if his request hadn't been bad enough, when I started to push back, he'd doubled down.

He got closer to my ear like he was sharing a secret. "Look, Esme. I know sometimes you're kind of uncertain about your writing."

*What?*

"So I'm here to help you," he continued.

"Um, Adam, I don't think that will be necessary, since I'm not doing the story."

He chuckled. "Now Esme, I know you want to excel here at the paper, and opportunities like this only come around once in a while. What I want you to really focus on is finding out more about his sister's death."

"*What?*" I snapped.

Matt gave me his usual warning look, which I normally heeded.

But not this time.

Adam held his hands up. "Okay. Okay, Esme. Just keep in mind that… another opportunity this *big* might not find its way to your desk for quite a long time."

Holy fuck. He was threatening me.

I stood up before I exploded, or burst into tears, or both. "I need to run to the ladies' room. I'll talk to you later."

I had to get away from him.

I locked the bathroom stall door behind myself and sat on the seat, head in hands.

Had I heard him right? Would he actually withhold assignments from me if I didn't write about Ty and his family?

I already knew the answer. Adam was just that petty and vindictive. I'd seen him mess with someone last year who finally gave up and surrendered, quitting in frustration. Something about refusing to 'stretch' the truth in a story he was working on.

While I sank into a new level of misery in one of the bathroom stalls, the outer door to the ladies' room blew open and two of my coworkers came in, chatting happily about their weekend plans. But then the subject changed.

"Hey, did you see that guy Esme brought to happy hour?" one of them said.

"Oh, hell yeah. How'd she land such a hottie?" the other said with a laugh.

"Seriously."

They giggled and left.

Way to go, universe. Any other shit you'd like to drop on my head before the day is over?

## 24

ESME

Thank goodness I was meeting the guys for dinner. I was desperate for a pick-me-up, and I knew they were just the ones to give it to me.

The second I walked into the restaurant and saw the guys already seated, watching me cross the room, my heart skipped a beat. There was nothing as comforting as seeing their handsome faces at the end of a shit day. Or any day.

"Hello, beautiful," Alden said, pulling out my chair for me.

I looked at each of them, one at a time. How'd I get so lucky to meet men like this, even if we were only going to be spending time together for the duration of my house fix-up.

They'd hinted at something longer term, but I just didn't see how that was supposed to work.

But for now, things were fine. We were all having fun with no expectation of anything further. And I planned to keep it that way.

The waiter happened by just as Case asked me what I wanted to drink.

"What are you guys having?" I asked.

Ty held up his glass. "Maker's Mark, baby. You want to join us?"

"No, no, no." I looked up at the waiter. "A glass of chardonnay for me, please."

Alden reached over and rubbed my back. "You okay, sweetie?"

My heart melted a little. Actually, a lot. It was so amazing to have someone looking out for me.

"It was an… interesting day at work."

Ty set down his drink. "Do you want to tell us about it?"

I thought for a moment. What the hell. I could be honest with these guys.

I rubbed my eyes before I spoke. "My boss, Adam—you met him at happy hour, Ty—came to me with a new writing assignment."

Ty rolled his eyes. "I can just imagine. Guys, you

need to get a load of this little weasel. He's as big a douchebag as they come."

Ty was about to become even less of an Adam fan.

"Well, he asked me to do a story on you, Ty, your family, and the death of your sister."

You could have heard a pin drop.

And poor Ty, his face paled as he absorbed the distastefulness of the idea.

Case looked down at the table. "Jesus Christ. He wants you to use your relationship with Ty that way?"

I didn't say anything. I didn't need to.

Until Ty looked at me with so much pain in his eyes I wanted to stab Adam in the heart. He'd never hurt Ty. At least not if I had anything to do with it.

"Are you… are you…?" Ty stumbled.

I reached for his hand. "Oh god no. I shut him down flat. I'd never do that, sweetie."

Relief washed over his face as he nodded slowly. "I'm sorry I asked. Of course you wouldn't. I know that."

"It's just really upsetting to know that I work for someone so horrible. And then he hinted around that if I didn't do this, it might impact my future work assignments."

Alden slammed his drink on the table. "You need to get a new job. That's all there is to it."

But Ty held a finger up. "Or… she could get rid of Adam."

Everyone looked at him.

"How do you propose to do that?" Case asked.

Ty smiled. "That Adam dude fucked with the wrong people. I might be semi-estranged from my family, but that doesn't mean our connections don't come in handy when I need them."

Oh my god. He was brilliant.

Fight fire with fire.

Why hadn't I thought of that?

I guess because I didn't realize I *had* fire.

AFTER WE'D FINISHED DESSERT, I yawned. It wasn't easy to keep up with these guys.

Alden stuffed his hands in his pockets as we stood out in front of the restaurant. "So where are we off to, now?"

Case shook his head. "I have an exam tomorrow. I gotta get home. You kids go ahead and have fun."

I watched him head for his car. Cripes, that guy had a lot on his plate with running a business and trying to finish his degree.

"Well," Alden said, "you two want to come over to my place for an after-dinner drink? Rosie's at my mom's for the night."

Ty and I looked at each other.

"Let's do it," I said.

I'd never been to Alden's place, and was psyched to see he had an adorable little bungalow with original wood trim, built-in cabinets, and a lovely fireplace. I could see that at one time the place was probably quite tidy with its dark, masculine furnishings, but now everywhere I looked, there was evidence that a baby had taken over his world.

I picked a teething ring up off the living room floor. "Did you drop something, Alden?" I asked, laughing.

He came over, put his arms around me, and lifted me off the floor. "I swear that's not mine. But you are," he said with a laugh.

Well.

He set me down in the middle of the living room, and he and Ty took seats as if they'd planned this.

"Um. What's going on?" I asked, standing before them, hands on hips.

Alden gave me a sly smile. "Nothing. We just want to see you undress."

Ty nodded in agreement.

They were serious.

And I was tempted. As they sat, their gazes heating me inside and out, I shifted on my feet, unable to hold as still as I would have liked. Standing before them was as torturous as being tickled with a feather, and I wanted to crawl right out of my skin.

These men were strong and powerful in their own right, with my red-headed Alden taking care of business by bringing up a little human, and Ty resisting his family money to pursue a talent that drove him to create incredible beauty.

How did I get so lucky to meet these two men, and how did I get so lucky that they liked *me*?

But why should I even ask myself that? I was a good person and deserved to be cared about by others.

So, fuck yeah, I would take off my clothes for these guys.

I began to sway my hips as Alden flicked on some music. "Hmmm. Where shall I start?"

Ty sat with his arms spread along the sofa back, one leg crossed over the other. "You decide, baby."

I kicked off my shoes and unzipped the back of my dress. Slipping it down my shoulders, I shimmied it past my hips and kicked it aside. I did a little turn for the guys in my lacy bra and thong panty.

I heard a low whistle and turned to find Alden nodding with approval. He looked over at Ty. "Dude, did you see that nice, juicy ass?"

Ty adjusted himself in his blue jeans. "Fuck yeah. I think it's time to bury my face in it, in fact. Why don't you come over here, baby?" he asked, crooking a finger.

I sauntered toward him, in no hurry to satisfy his demand. But when I was within his reach, he spun me around so I faced away, and with his hands on my hips, pulled me close until my ass was right in his face.

"Lean forward, baby," he rasped.

So I did, and next I knew, he'd pulled aside the narrow strip of my thong and started to lick me *back there*.

And holy mother of god did it feel great.

"Didn't know you were an ass man, Ty," Alden said.

His face buried between my cheeks, he mumbled something neither of us could make out. But it didn't matter. He got the message across.

Alden pushed an ottoman in my direction and when it was in front of me, instructed me to bend forward even farther by placing my hands on it. This put my ass more squarely in Ty's face. He groaned and licked me from behind with even more passion.

In the meantime, with one hand I reached for Alden's fly and through a tangle of jeans and boxers, got my hand around his erect cock. He moaned at my touch and sucked his breath when I licked a drop of precum from the tip.

There was a rustling behind me, and I realized Ty was opening his jeans. While I played with Alden's cock, he reached down to play with my breasts.

"I'd like to fuck you, baby," he said.

"Yeah. Do it, Ty."

I heard plastic tearing behind me and a condom being rolled on. Ty positioned himself at my opening.

At the same time, I pulled Alden deep into my mouth until he banged the back of my throat, then pulled him back out again to run my tongue around the ridge of his swollen cock head.

In a slow but steady thrust, Ty was inside me, filling my pussy to its limits, his hands gripping my hips tightly. He rocked me back and forth, his cock sliding in and out, and Alden's hard dick doing the same in my mouth.

It was perfect. The three of us shared a rhythm that hummed through my body, invaded on both ends by two amazing guys.

My orgasm started with a tickle and built until it left my legs trembling and my breaths coming in short gasps, even with my mouth full of Alden's cock. Then, just as he started to spurt in my mouth, I exploded with a sensation that shook me from head to toe.

With a loud grunt, Ty pushed deep inside me one last time and held himself there, throbbing against the walls of my pussy.

The guys straightened my bent body upright and the two of them half-carried me up the stairs to Alden's room. With a glance over my shoulder, I smiled as I noted the hard wood floor of his living room littered in clothing, as if three people had just had a very good time.

25

## CASE

I couldn't remember ever having been so pissed off about… well, everything.

Just when I thought things were finally falling into place, I found they weren't. I was back at square one and possibly even worse off than before. If that were possible.

Which I knew, it was.

It didn't help that this was my college buddies' weekend away. They were having fun. I didn't know that because I was there with them, participating and having a great time. Rather, I knew they always had fun when they were together, and my not joining them because of the mountain of shit I had raining down on my head pissed me the hell off.

I was in the office on a Saturday. With my mother. If anyone had asked me up till the moment my father died whether I wanted to join the family business and work with either or both of my parents, my answer would have started out by laughing out loud, and then been followed by a *fuck no*.

And yet.

My mom barged into my office.

Just like she always did.

"Honey," she started as she helped herself to a seat in my office. Well, it was actually her office, too.

I stuffed the English exam I was looking at into my desk drawer and folded my hands on my desk.

"Hey, Mom."

She shuffled together a pile of the papers she'd brought in with her. "Where are we with the old Buckner house?

For a moment, Esme's face flashed through my mind. And for a moment, everything seemed better.

But only for a moment.

"You need to come over there with me, Mom. It's looking good. Much better than it was. But hey, it's no longer the old Buckner house. It belongs to Esme Rutherford now."

As if Mom didn't know that.

She sighed impatiently. "The reason I'm checking is

that the mayor wants the work done on his house sooner rather than later. You need to put the Buckner... I mean, Esme's house on hold."

Was she fucking kidding? You never stopped in the middle of a project. Well, unless the money ran out.

And in this case, there was no money, anyway.

"Mom, we can't do that. It would be a shitty move."

"I'm sorry, Case, but we have the chance to make some good money with a very high-profile client. Either finish up Esme's house, or find a good stopping point. You can always go back to it later. Or just finish it on weekends."

She had a point. But I just couldn't bail on Esme.

I'd grown attached to that project... and to her.

There were mornings I woke up when the only thing I looked forward to was her coming home at the end of the day and seeing the progress we'd made on her house. The thought of not having that was... well, unfathomable.

It was funny. The more time I spent with her, the more I thought I *might* remember her from high school. There were flashes of familiarity, but never anything very clear. But I'd been so wrapped up with my buddies and sports back then, it was amazing I'd even graduated.

It would have been nice to know her better in high school.

Mom leaned on my desk and looked at me with

raised eyebrows. "If I didn't know better, Case, I'd swear you were a little sweet on her."

If she only knew.

I sat back in my chair and shrugged. "I do like her, Mom. We've become… friends. She's a really cool girl. But look, I know Dad did things differently than I do. But that didn't make him a good businessman. I mean, look at the condition of our books."

"Well, that's not exactly—"

"I know he meant well, but his kind of operation burned bridges. I'm trying to establish a better reputation for McKinney Construction. I'll call the mayor and let him know he's next on our list."

Mom pressed her lips into a thin line. "You know, he might just go to another builder if he has to wait."

I nodded, somehow buoyed by having made a definitive decision. "I know there's the possibility of that. But after I talk to him, I think we'll be fine."

She sniffed. "Well, just watch out for her. I know how girls like her are—"

"*Mom*," I interrupted. "Whatever you think you know about her is probably wrong."

"Well, you know, her own mother—"

"Mom, Esme's mother is not in the picture."

I was inches from telling her to *back the fuck off*, but I resisted the thought of speaking to my mother that way. However, we were business partners and needed to be straight with each other.

"Case, you don't have to—"

"Mom, I am doing all I can for our business and our family. Dad left us with a mess that I'm trying to clean up while finishing my degree and having some modicum of a life. I'm sticking with our commitments and that means finishing with Esme's house first. Now, I'd like to finish the last of this paperwork so I can get out of here and enjoy the rest of my Saturday."

She nodded. "Fine."

If I were so sure I was doing the right thing, then why did I feel so shitty?

CASE

"Whoa. You scared the crap out of me."

Putting down her paintbrush, Esme playfully pushed me in the chest after I'd grabbed her from behind. She leaned to give me a kiss, transferring the smudge of paint on her nose to my own.

A kiss from her was worth the mess and I wanted a lot more of where that came from. But I could be patient.

To a point.

I picked up a rag and scrubbed the paint off her face and she did the same for me. "I was at the office this morning. I'd had enough of work, and… realized I really wanted to see you."

She beamed. "That is the nicest thing I think I've heard since… well, maybe forever."

"So you're painting the kitchen," I said, examining her work.

She grabbed the paint roller to fill in one last swath of wall. "Well, Ty's new cabinets are looking so awesome, I thought a fresh coat of paint was in order. Doesn't it look amazing?"

Those couple things really did make a difference. And even better, I could see Esme was thrilled.

She deserved a break.

"I'd really been tempted to paint the kitchen turquoise, my favorite color, but I know white is best for selling a house. So I made an adult decision for a change."

I loved a woman who could laugh at herself.

And when I thought about it, I couldn't remember the last time I'd known one.

She washed her hands and when she realized she had nothing to dry them with, wiped them down the front of her T-shirt.

"Hey, let me show you what we're doing in the little room." I led her by the hand, and when we entered, I got on my knees to show her how we were filling the cracks in the old plaster walls.

She ran her hand over our work. "It's so smooth.

You'd never know how lumpy this wall had been just one week ago. You guys are so awesome," she said, her eyes getting watery. "I don't know how I'll ever repay you."

I could think of a few ways…

*Down, boy.*

She joined me where I had just sat on the floor. "This is such a teeny little room. I've wondered what it was designed to be."

I looked around, trying to imagine the original purpose of the room whose walls had been stained and cracked until we got to work on it. "Might have been built to be a nursery back in the day."

She brushed her fingers over my hand on the floor, and I swear to god, I felt a calm begin to wash over me.

"I… I got my English exam back."

Her eyes widened. "Oh my god. Tell me. Did you ace it?"

Fuck. Why did I even bring it up?

I shook my head slowly. "No. I wasn't as well-prepared as I should have been. I could have done better."

She ran a hand up my arm. "Don't feel badly. It's only one test. You still have your final exam and your term paper."

She was right. But I guess what bummed me out the most was the knowledge that with my responsibilities to the business, I just didn't have the time I needed to dedicate to school. Sure, I was going to pass my classes. But I needed to do better than that if I wanted to get into graduate school.

"You amaze me," Esme said, putting her hand on my chin and turning my face toward hers.

"Huh?"

"Look at you. Taking over the family business when it was about the last thing in the world you wanted to do, looking out for your mom, plugging away at school. Helping me out, although I have no idea why you'd waste your time doing that…"

Was she fucking kidding? She was pretty much the only ray of sunshine in my life at the moment.

And then she got real with me.

She looked down at our touching hands. "You're nothing like you were in high school."

Oh. Shit.

"Esme, how did we know each other back then?"

I felt like she knew something I didn't, and that wasn't a good thing.

She looked up at me. "You and I once… made out under the bleachers."

I dropped my head back and laughed. "No way. We did?"

Her serious expression indicated we sure had.

"Not so hilarious, really. You told your friends, who then told everyone in school. I had the distinct pleasure of being the school slut for a week or so, until some new, juicier gossip replaced my story."

Holy fuck. I remembered her now. I'd been so pissed my friends blabbed but had been too much of a jerk to stop them.

Yeah, I'd been a head-up-my-ass teenager more concerned with what my friends thought than anything or anyone else.

And now I could see the damage I caused. Shame hit me like a speeding truck, and I knew I deserved every bit of the discomfort that brought with it.

"Holy shit. You were that girl? You don't look anything like—"

She stopped me. "Yeah, I know. I don't look much like I did in high school. When I got to college, I ditched the glasses and got in shape taking dance classes. Kind of reinvented myself."

I looked at Esme, this amazing woman, helping me out of my funk, whom I'd once hurt.

"Jesus, Esme. I'm so sorry. And I know I don't deserve it, but I hope you can forgive me—"

She held a hand up. "I've already forgiven you. In fact, I forgave you when it happened. It was an asshole teenage boy thing. You're not that kid anymore, just like I'm not that girl anymore."

Fuck me. I could learn from her grace. Maybe if I stopped resenting where I was in life and changed how I looked at things, I'd begin to be more like her.

"You… dazzle me," I said, running a long strand of her hair through my fingers.

God, that sounded fucking lame.

But whatever.

I lay back on the drop cloth covering the floor and pulled her on top of me. I ground my hard cock against her pussy through our blue jeans as I unbuttoned hers and she made fast work of mine.

I reached into my pocket for a condom and pushed my jeans down below my ass while she shook free of one leg of her own. I sheathed myself, and Esme hovered over my hard dick.

"Kiss me first," I demanded.

She leaned down and as our lips brushed and then pressed furiously, I held her hips and slowly lowered her on my erection. She gasped as I filled her, and once I was all the way inside, she straightened up and threw her head back.

With her hands on my chest for balance, she began to rock. I reached up for her delicious tits, and after smoothing my palms over her hard nipples, I tweaked them between my fingers until she moaned.

"So… fucking… hot…" I groaned, the pressure in my balls building to the point of pain.

"Oh… oh… fuck me, Case," she cried, her head bucking as she rode me harder and harder.

Her pussy clamped around my dick and she came hard, hair flying, her nails leaving marks on my chest.

With one final thrust upward, I emptied my load in pulsing releases, all my concerns of the day gone while every bit of my energy focused on the beautiful woman straddling me.

I pulled her down on top of me so the crusty drop cloth didn't scrape her skin, and wished for a split second I could go back to high school and do things differently.

## 27

ESME

"FRANCESCA, THERE IS NO WAY I COULD ACCEPT THIS."

Charli's mom shook her head and smiled. This was our thing. She offered me something outrageously expensive from *To Die For*, which I could never afford, and I protested.

And in the end, always accepted.

Charli play slapped me on the arm. "Don't be ridonculous. Mom's offering you that kick ass blouse, so freaking accept it. Girl, it's the only way we're gonna have expensive stuff like this."

I threw my arms around Francesca, who'd been, on many occasions, the mom I never had.

"Thank you," I murmured into her perfectly blown-out hair.

"You're welcome, honey. Now, Char, what are you choosing as your little gift from me? And don't say that dress over there. I have a paying customer who has her eye on it. She's supposed to come in tomorrow and pay for it in *cash*."

Charli fingered a pair of palazzo pants. "Cash. Well, I sure can't compete with that." She pulled the pants out and held them to her waist in front of a full-length mirror.

When Francesca offered us a gift from *To Die For*, Charli always chose something she'd never actually wear. It was baffling. I mean, where the hell would she ever get to use palazzo pants? Actually, where the hell did *anyone* wear palazzo pants?

And yet she had a closet full of floofy stuff like that.

If she ever became some rich man's wife and turned into a lady of leisure, I suppose she'd have luncheons and the opera and shit like that to attend. But until that happened, she had a fuck ton of expensive clothes in her closet collecting dust.

But that was on her.

I nudged her to move along. We were supposed to spend the day thrifting in a place where we could actually afford to buy things, and I wanted to get on with it without giving Francesca the bum's rush. Sure, the stuff we picked up during our shopping sprees was all second-hand, but we'd honed our skills and knew where and when to go for the good stuff.

For example, the local Value Village put all their new clothing out on the floor every Saturday morning. You bet your ass we were down there several times a month waiting for them to open. And we weren't the only ones.

There was a whole subculture of people who lived to thrift. It was almost as much of a hobby as a way to freshen up one's wardrobe.

We didn't talk about it much in front of Francesca. She didn't get the appeal of finding a good deal on something.

But as Charli loaded up and headed to the dressing room, I realized we were not leaving anytime soon. I settled into the sofa where the bored husbands usually hung out and flipped through a magazine on cigars.

Francesca's idea of what men waiting for their women liked to read.

After she rang up a customer's purchase and walked the woman to the door, she came over and grabbed a seat next to me.

"So how're you doing, honey. You know, with all the stuff?"

'Stuff' being her euphemism for being stood up at the altar and the fall-out that came with it.

It was funny. I hadn't actually, really, thought about how I was doing in a couple days. I took that as a good sign. I was no longer vacillating between the sadness of what might have been and the anger of how things turned out. Things were just as they were. Like I'd accepted them and moved on.

Is that even possible?

'Course, none of this would have happened without the guys.

I should write an article for *City Scene* about getting over your shit by having a fling with three guys who, by the way, were good friends *and* worked together. I could see it now.

*Forget all your troubles and get laid at the same time.*

Yeah, no.

As it was, I was still trying to figure out how to manage my asshole boss's expectation that I was going to write some sort of tell-all about Ty and his family.

Francesca put a hand over mine. "I know it hasn't been easy, sweetie," she said, pushing a lock of hair out of my face.

I wanted to close my eyes and ask her to do that a hundred more times. That's what growing up without a mom was like. The craving for one never ended.

"Do you remember much about my mom?"

She nodded slowly. "I do. And I think about her a lot. She was my best friend."

Well, until she took off to Mexico with a surfer, leaving Dad holding the bag. And me.

"You look more like her every year."

I took that as a compliment. Everyone always raved about what a beauty my mom was. On one hand it's not easy hearing praise of a mother who takes off on you, but there it was.

"So how's the house coming?"

Ah, the house. What was once an albatross was becoming a joy. I hadn't seen that coming. I didn't suppose anyone did.

"Well, it still needs tons more work, but I think we're getting it to a point where we can sell it without taking a loss. Because you know, my dad loaned me the money for the down payment. I want to return to him at least what he gave me."

Charli joined us in a sequined evening gown.

Was she fucking kidding?

"Yeah, how is the house?" she asked, turning in the three-fold mirror to see her butt.

"You know, I'm kind of getting to where I wish I could stay there, if you can believe it. I've developed quite an affection for the place."

"That's not the only thing she's developed an affection for," Charli said.

The stink eye I threw shut her right up.

"There's this tiny room on the second floor, right next to the master bedroom. I think it might have been a nursery at one time."

Charli's mouth dropped open. "Oh. My. God. She's talking about *babies*."

Francesca shook her head. "Nothing wrong with that, Charli."

"But, Mom, she hates kids. We both do. We've vowed to never have kids."

Francesca laughed. "At your age, you are entitled to change your mind."

Charli screwed up her face at me and huffed back to the dressing room.

Jesus. I had no idea I was incriminating myself just talking about a nursery. Fine.

I wouldn't bring it up again.

Nor would I tell her how baby Rosie was more beautiful in person than in a photo on her father's phone.

"Was that more painful than usual, or am I just PMSing?"

Matt looked around to make sure Adam was nowhere in the vicinity as we returned to our cubes. "I think that staff meeting was definitely an outlier. Something's going on."

Shit. Shit, shit, shit.

I didn't like it when *things were going on*. They always rattled me into thinking my employment was coming to an end.

And since I'd started lying to Adam, I'd become more paranoid than ever.

Just before the morning's meeting, he took me aside. I was certain he was going to ask me to do an update on next week's staff retreat, but he had something else in mind.

"What's up with the story about the Wells family?" he asked, his eyes laced with evil enthusiasm.

Fucker didn't understand the meaning of the word no. It was like he just went deaf the moment I began pushing back on his stupid-ass idea and tried to explain how it wouldn't work.

It was quite a skill, not hearing what you didn't want to hear.

But this time I knew to stall. Buy myself some time. I had to figure out how to handle this, since there was no way he was going to back off.

"Um, yeah, Adam, I've um... started. Sure," I lied.

I was a terrible liar.

But he wanted this so badly he either didn't notice or didn't care. His face lit up. "Oh great. This is going to be wonderful for the paper. When can I see a draft?"

Shit.

"Oh, I don't have a draft for you yet. I'm still... interviewing people. You know, I had to sell the idea. At first the Wells weren't into it. But now I think they are."

He frowned. "You *think* they are? Or they *are*?"

"They *are*. Yup. For sure." I nodded like a bobble head.

He patted me on the back. "Super," he crowed, and hustled to the head of the room where he could address his team.

"I heard you bullshitting Adam," Matt whispered.

"I know," I whispered back. "I don't know what I'm going to do."

Seriously. I was not writing a story about a guy I was sleeping with. Hell, even if I weren't sleeping with him, I would not write a story about him or his family. There was no news there—Adam was just looking for salacious gossip.

And that was not something he'd ever get from me.

The only thing was, I had to figure out how to shut him down *and* keep my job. I wasn't sure I could pull off both.

## 28

## ALDEN

"Alden Pierce here."

The car behind me beeped angrily, drowning out my attempt to answer in incoming call.

I'd been stopped at a red light, staring at a snapshot my mom had taken of Rosie and me, which I'd taped to my dashboard. It was simple and at the same time the most beautiful thing I'd ever seen. Rosie had one finger in her drooly mouth as she looked up at me, her little eyes crinkling with laughter. And then there were the wisps of her crazy red hair. My mother had assured me it would fill in soon. But I didn't care what her hair looked like.

She was my Rosie.

When the beeping stopped, I tried again. "Hello, this is Alden Pierce here."

I inched forward in the heavy traffic.

"Hello, Alden. It's Ted over at Troy and Sons."

Huh. McKinney's biggest competitor. But it was a friendly competition.

Most of the time.

"Hey, Ted. How are things over there?"

His voice boomed with a deep laugh. "Great, Alden. Really great. We're growing leaps and bounds since we did the downtown project."

Right. That was a piece of business I was sure Case would have liked to bid on. But he'd said McKinney wasn't ready for commercial work. He wanted to keep the company residential for the time being. I'd tried to change his mind until he elaborated on the company's financial situation and explained he preferred we not take on any major risk until our debt was paid down.

"Well, good for you guys," I said. "You deserve every success that comes your way. You all worked very hard for it."

"Speaking of hard work," Ted said, "what do you think of joining our team?"

Okay, I was not expecting *that*.

"You got me there, Ted. I'm… speechless," I said, stalling for time.

"Look, Alden, we know you've been with McKinney

a long time. You're a top-notch builder. You should come over to a company that has a... shall we say... good reputation."

Holy shit. Did he really just say that?

"Ted, not sure where you're getting your information—"

But he cut me off. "Alden, word on the street is that McKinney is struggling to pay its bills. Something about debt left by the old man."

Fuck. I knew this was the case. But how did it become public information?

I was at a loss for words. "I'm, um, honored, Ted. Can I give it some thought?"

"Of course, Alden," he boomed. "Let's try for lunch next week then."

I was flattered. I couldn't lie.

But leave McKinney?

It was unfathomable.

But Ted had a point. If the company were in that much trouble, well that didn't bode well for my becoming a partner or even continuing employment.

There was a time when I would have told someone like Ted to take a hike. But I had a responsibility to Rosie, and an even greater one with her mother out of the picture. My relatively new craving for a certain amount of stability overrode how I used to live my life. Under the circumstances, I guess that was a good thing.

Life was strange. But what wasn't strange was my attraction to the lovely Esme.

I was going to be seeing her in a matter of minutes, and I wasn't sure if it was the call from Ted or the anticipation of seeing her that gave me a surge of energy, but the challenges of the day seemed a little less burdensome.

I WALKED into Esme's house, where I'd already spent the better part of my day. But it was different now. Instead of the roar of saws and pounding of hammers, it was full of the smells of delicious cooking. And laughter.

The best part was that Esme was there.

"Alden!" she cried, running to throw her arms around me.

How did this woman know exactly what I needed, when I needed it?

I held her for a moment longer than was necessary, not that anyone was complaining, and buried my nose in her thick hair, which smelled of nothing more than simple soap and shampoo. Exactly how I liked it.

I pulled back, still holding her, to take in her beautiful smile, and if I weren't mistaken, a small bead of sweat on her upper lip.

"Hot in the kitchen?" I asked.

She dabbed her face with her sleeve and giggled. "So hot. I accidentally painted the windows shut. But wait till you see what I'm making for dinner."

I followed her to the kitchen where she'd put Case and Ty to work. We didn't have much left to do on the house, and Esme had insisted on making dinner for us to celebrate.

"Check out what's in the oven, Alden," Case said, gesturing while he snapped a large bowl of green beans.

I pulled the oven door open a couple inches and found a big, fat, roast chicken in the final stages of cooking.

"Hurry up with those beans, Case. The sauté pan is already hot," Esme called.

I put the beer I'd brought in the fridge. "What can I do to help?"

"Oh, my dad loaned me his card table. It's in the living room with fold-up chairs. Would you set it all up for me?" she asked, smiling.

Shit, I'd do anything that woman asked me.

Twenty minutes later we were sitting down to an incredible meal on a rickety card table set up in Esme's still-under-construction living room. Since no lighting had been installed yet, she'd bought string lights and hung them around the room, giving it a festive glow, and set up clusters of candles in each corner. 'Rustic chic' was what she'd called it.

I liked it. A lot. It was just so… Esme.

After dinner we guys were kicking back with glasses of scotch for ourselves and a champagne for Esme, when I figured I'd start clearing the table. I needed to pick up Rosie from my mom's before it got too late.

When I got back to the living room, I found Esme straddling Ty where he sat, with Case behind her, reaching around to cup her breasts under her shirt.

Fuck yeah.

Her eyes were closed, and her head dropped back.

That's what I'm talking about.

"Alden, c'mon over," Case said, gesturing with his chin.

He and Ty let go of Esme and helped her to her feet.

"Esme was just telling us she wanted something from you," Case said.

I walked over to our girl and held her chin between my fingers. "Hey, gorgeous. Do you need what I think you do?"

She batted her eyes at me. "What do you think I need?" she asked coyly.

I pulled her T-shirt over her head and tossed it aside. Then, I put my hands on either side of her face and pulled her in for a kiss.

But before our lips touched, I whispered in her ear. "I think baby wants some dick."

Breaking into a huge smile, she pushed her jeans

down and kicked them aside. "Do you have a condom?" she asked.

"Of course," I said, pulling one from my pocket.

"Way to go," Ty said, laughing.

"Somebody was a Boy Scout in a previous life," Case added.

"You know it," I said as Esme made quick work of my belt and jeans. "Come over here, baby," I said as soon as I'd kicked aside my clothes.

I placed her hands on the back of one of the folding chairs and bent her at a ninety-degree angle so her ass was pretty much in the air. Then I positioned myself right behind her.

"Are you ready for me, baby?" I asked.

Tossing her hair around, she wiggled her ass against me. "Yeah, Alden. I'm ready."

I plunged inside her until my balls smacked her clit, and holding myself there, reveled in the grip of her pussy on my stiff cock.

Pumping her slowly, I ran my thumb over her pink asshole. When she moaned, I took it as my cue to explore further.

Wetting my thumb, I gently pushed it past her tight ring. She gasped and pushed back against me.

"Nice," Case murmured, playing with her tits and stroking himself.

A quick glance at Ty showed me he was doing the same.

Esme reached for his cock. Pulling him towards her, she wrapped her lips around him and sucked.

His head fell back, and he moaned, gripping her hair to drive himself deeper.

Goddamn, this woman was hot.

I pushed my thumb deeper in her ass while pistoning her pussy. My balls began to tighten as I got ready to shoot my load.

At the same time, Ty groaned, thrusting himself deeply into Esme's mouth one last time, presumably unloading his own explosion down her throat.

He pulled out of her mouth in time for her to buck her head and shudder while an orgasm rolled over her.

That was all I needed.

I started to pump my cum inside her with every ounce of energy I had, ramming her pussy over and over until she was weak from my fucking.

I caught her as her shaking legs gave out, and pulled her to me for that kiss I meant to grab earlier. She was soft and pliant under me. Our fit was perfect.

Actually, more than perfect.

29

———————

**ESME**

*B*AM, BAM, BAM.

Who was banging on my door at the crack of dawn?

I slid my feet into my scuffs and pulled a sweatshirt over my nightie.

I hoped it wasn't a neighbor complaining about the construction, or worse, the general appearance of the exterior of the house.

Although it was a lot better than it had been just a few weeks before.

And then another thought stopped me mid-stairs. My heart began to pound as the panic set in.

What if it was the bank? The fucking bank. Did they

even operate that way, showing up at your house unannounced, asking for either their money or you to vacate the house they were foreclosing on?

Could they just show up and kick my sorry ass out?

I'd never heard of anything like that, but banks were such dicks, who the hell knew?

I grabbed my phone but wasn't even sure whom to call.

My dad? Cripes, I couldn't bother him with any more of my problems.

Charli? She'd come over, guns a-blazing, and probably get us both thrown in jail.

One or all of the guys? They'd know what to do—

"Open up, Esme. I can hear you in there!" a voice boomed, pounding on the door.

Holy shit. Was that Eddie?

I yanked the door open. "What are you doing here?" I asked, too shocked to even consider whether I should be polite or rude.

I'd not laid eyes on him since our rehearsal dinner, the night before the wedding-that-wasn't.

He had new glasses. A new haircut. And an expensive-looking new suit.

Nice that he was living so well.

He started to cross the threshold when I put my hand on his chest.

"No, no, no. You don't just get to walk in here," I said, trying to fill the doorway with my frame.

He dutifully took a step back and held his hands up in surrender. "Okay. Okay. But don't forget, I'm half owner of this house, too."

Was he really going there?

"Yeah, half owner of a house you dumped on me, and which you've contributed nothing to get it fixed up for sale."

He put his hands on his hips and looked down at his polished wing tips. "I know. I know all that Esme. I've caught the house up on the mortgage payments. But I have more to talk to you about than that."

I raised my eyebrows, waiting for him to continue.

Looking back at me, his mouth trembled. "I... I made a mistake, Esme. I did a horrible thing in calling off the wedding. And I'm so, so sorry." His voice caught as he stifled a sob.

Holyfuckingshit. Was he for real?

I just kept staring at him, trying to assess whether he was full of it or being sincere.

He took a deep breath to compose himself. "Can we... can we just talk?"

Well, shit. I didn't have to be at work for almost three hours, he'd woken me up so early.

"Would you like to come in for some coffee?"

He smiled gratefully and followed me into the house.

"Holy shit. This place is looking amazing," he said, walking around in wonder. "And look at the goddamn kitchen. What happened to the old cabinets?"

"McKinney Construction is doing the work on the house including the kitchen. It's not a total renovation, since *I* don't have the money for that, but they're fixing up a few things that should help it sell." I stood back next to him as he gazed at Ty's gorgeous woodwork.

"What a transformation. It's incredible how a few things can make such a difference." He turned toward me.

And was standing uncomfortably close.

"Esme. I want to try again. I want *us* to try again. I've… missed you so much. I've just been miserable."

He had a funny way of showing it.

"Eddie, last time we spoke you threatened to sell the house out from under me. On top of that, I heard you had some new woman already. What the hell are you up to?"

He looked impatient at my questioning, but then shook it off. "Esme, I've been to therapy. And the other woman is gone. She wasn't right for me."

Okay, pretty sure that was a bold-faced lie. But I let him continue.

"You don't believe me. I can see that. And I don't blame you. But I'm here to try to atone for my mistakes. My horrible, regretful mistakes. I've missed you so much. I've been miserable. I haven't been sleeping, and my work has suffered. I might even get... fired."

He was really laying it on.

"I miss your voice and your smiles, and your kindness. Your dedication to the paper, your father, and your friends. I miss your smart-ass attitude—"

"I thought that bugged you," I interrupted.

He held his hands up. "It did. But then I realized I respected it."

*Respect.* He knew that was the magic word with me. Dammit.

Now I was beginning to feel for him. He did look miserable. Shit.

And next thing I knew, he'd pulled me to him, his lips pressing mine softly. He pulled back slightly, as if to gauge my reaction, and when I didn't push him away, he kissed me with more passion.

I couldn't deny it. I'd always been rendered paralyzed by Eddie's kisses. It used to be, when we were together, that all he had to do was kiss me and I'd be begging him for sex. Even though he wasn't much into it.

Fucking strange.

But the hold he'd once had on me?

Gone.

His kiss was as interesting as one of Adam's staff meetings. Maybe even less so.

"Oh. Oh shit. Sorry. Didn't mean to intrude."

I looked up to see Case hightailing it out of the kitchen, his face covered in surprise.

"Wait, Case!" I called, but he'd grabbed his tools and headed to the back of the house.

Shit. I'd forgotten all about the morning arrivals of the guys. Jesus. Where was my head?

I put my hands on Eddie and steered him toward the door. "You need to leave. Now," I hissed.

As we neared the door, he stopped. "Please, Esme. Give me another chance."

I nodded to get rid of him. "I… I'll think about it, Eddie. I'll call you later. Or tomorrow," I lied.

"Esme, I love you. I really do."

Shit.

I pushed the door closed after him and turned to find Case standing there, watching.

## 30

## ESME

"YOU KNOW, YOU CAN ORDER SOME FRIES OF YOUR OWN."

Charli narrowed her eyes and taunted me by swiping not one but two more fries off my plate.

She always did this. Claimed fries were way too unhealthy. Then ate half of mine.

I supposed she was doing me a favor by leaving only half of them for me to consume.

"Here, Charli, you can have some of mine. I ordered the large," Matt said.

Charli shimmied her shoulders in victory and dug in.

I had to keep from laughing.

"So tell me, Es. You always say Matt is your 'work husband.' Does that mean you guys go at it in the storage closet when no one is around?"

Matt rolled his eyes. "Yeah, Charli, that's just what it means. You've got us figured out."

"Don't be an idiot," I said, pushing the rest of my fries towards her. "It just means your best work friend is someone of the opposite sex."

She looked between the two of us, eating our fries and doubting our claims.

"Maybe if you got a job someday, you'd know what we mean," Matt said.

Oh no he didn't.

Charli stiffened. "I'll have you know, I do have a job at my mom's boutique. She pays me… in clothes."

Not a bad way to be paid, if you asked me, but pretty clothes didn't cover food and rent. Or a mortgage in my case. Charli was lucky her mother was a champ at marrying rich men.

I tilted my head at her. "Char, Matt meant the kind of job you have to *show up at* every now and then. When was the last time you worked at *To Die For?*"

She screwed up her face, thinking. "Well, I was there just the other day with you—"

"Yeah, but we were trying on clothes. Not working."

She threw her hands up in the air. "All right. Fine. I

go in when Mom needs help. It's been kind of slow lately since we're in between seasons. When Christmas rolls around, though, I'll be in there every day."

She sighed like she was already tired.

"So, guys, you'll never guess who I saw this morning," I said.

"I'll guess you're not going to say one of your construction guys, because you see them every day, anyway," Matt said.

I touched my finger to my nose. "You are correct."

Charli's eye suddenly widened. "Did your very handsome and very available father happen to stop by, and if so, why didn't you call me right away?" She drummed her fingers on the table.

I gave her a look. "No, my father didn't stop by, and what would be noteworthy about that, anyway?"

She shrugged.

"Okay, since you both are too lame to guess, it was Eddie. Eddie stopped by."

They both set their food down and stared.

"No fucking way."

"Are you kidding?"

"I am not kidding, my friends. And he wants to get back together."

Charli slammed her hand on the table so hard all heads turned in our direction in the overcrowded lunch diner.

"I *told* you he'd come crawling back around," she said, shaking a finger in my face. "So what are you going to do?" she asked with wide eyes.

"Well, Eddie could solve a lot of my problems, not least of which is taking care of the freaking house. I'd be back in a steady relationship—"

"What is it about women and their goddamned need for 'relationships'?" Matt said, interrupting me with air quotes.

Charli and I gave him a look that shut him right up.

"Jesus, guys, don't worry. I'm not getting back with him. In fact, I need to call him later. Putting him off was the only way I could get him out of the house."

"He was in your *house*?" Charli hissed.

I nodded. "And he kissed me just when Case was arriving."

"Case saw?" Charli asked, her eyes widening.

"Yeah. I didn't have a chance to talk to him before I left for work. Not that I even know what to say, anyway. But, you know, I can't be with those guys. I mean, how does a woman date three men?"

Matt scoffed. "If there were three women who wanted to date me, you'd best believe I'd find a way to make it work. Fuck everybody else. I'd kill for my own harem."

Oh my god. That's what it was. A harem.

But I shook the thought away. "I just don't see how it would work. And I'll admit I imagined being with

Eddie again. Just for a split second. But I can't be with him, either. So I'll just have to be alone."

Charli and Matt looked at each other and shrugged.

"Well. If that's what you really want."

The problem is, I didn't know what I wanted.

## 31

## TY

"Goddammit."

I looked over toward Case, but I wasn't going to ask him what was up his ass again. He'd been throwing shit around all day and swearing, but wouldn't breathe a word of what was going on with either Alden or me. It must have been a biggie.

But he was a big boy. He'd talk to us when he was ready.

All I did know was that when I arrived at work that morning and Esme was heading out the door, she'd hollered goodbye and for everyone to have a nice day.

He was the only one who didn't answer.

So my guess was that something happened between them. And I guessed I'd find out about it sooner or later.

I was both glad and sad that we were finishing our work on Esme's house. I know she needed us to finish up so she could unload it, but I had to admit coming to work every day in the place where she lived felt... comfortable. It made me happy.

And I was even happier when she got home at the end of every day.

Now, that chapter was coming to a close. But it could mean a new one was starting.

Besides, we had to get working on the pain-in-the-ass-mayor's house. He'd been hounding Case to start his reno. Unbelievably, when he'd been told the team wasn't available until we finished our current project, he'd called Case's *mother*.

Yup. He'd actually called Mrs. McKinney. Like Case was some sort of bad kid he could get in trouble.

He almost came to know how that move had backfired on him. But Mrs. McKinney had kept Case from going over to his house and punching him right in the nose.

Yeah, that would not have been good.

Poor Case. The truth was, he was not cut out for this business, but he was trapped in it, nonetheless.

We all had our crosses to bear. And it seemed like

the load of carrying one of mine just might become lighter.

One of my mother's friends from the club, a well-known interior designer, had seen a write-up somewhere about my award-winning chair design. That had sparked a call from my mom, something that rarely happened.

I'd grabbed the phone on the first ring. My mother called so seldom I figured it had to be some sort of emergency. And as much as I was on the outs with my father, my stomach dropped when I thought something might have happened to him.

"Tyler? It's your mother."

"I know it's you, Mom. What happened? Is everything all right?" I blurted.

She clucked her tongue. "Honey, calm down. Of course, everything is all right. Why wouldn't it be?"

I thought of going down the road of reminding her that I was pretty much estranged from Dad and her for several reasons, not limited to the death of her daughter and my chosen career, and that it was out of the ordinary for her to just pick up the phone and call.

But I decided to save that for another day.

"Sounds good, Mom. So what's up with you?"

She laughed lightly. "Well, maybe *I* should be asking, what's up with *you*?"

What the hell was she talking about?

"Um, not sure, Mom. Nothing much. Just working on a house with Case and Alden."

I could picture her sitting in the solarium, her favorite room in the house, her blonde hair perfectly coiffed thanks to her weekly hairdresser appointments, her skin perfectly smoothed, thanks to the best plastic surgeon money could buy. She was a trophy wife, no two ways about it.

And while I loved my mother, she sure as hell wasn't the type of woman I pictured myself with in the long term.

"Silly. I heard about your chair. And the award."

Oh. That.

"Right! Isn't it cool? Such an honor. How'd you find out?"

"Oh, one of the girls at the club read it in an interior design magazine. I'm very proud of you, honey."

I slipped outside to get away from Case's swearing and slamming things around. Jesus, he had a real bug up his ass.

"You know, I think your father is finally seeing why you do the work you do," she said.

No way. The stubborn old man never changed his position on things. With him, reflection was a weakness.

"Well, Mom, that's nice of you to say, but I don't think Dad's changing his position on his feelings about me—"

But she didn't want to hear it. Had she been plan-ning some way to bring me back into the family fold all along, waiting for the right excuse?

"Ty, honey, can you come over for dinner next week?"

Okay, now I was officially confused.

"Um, yeah. Sure," I stumbled.

"If it's not too much trouble, can you bring the chair? I want your father to see it. And I think my inte-rior designer friend wants to use it for one of her hotel projects."

Holy shit. No fucking way.

Someone wanted to buy my chair? Or rather, multi-ples of it?

I was far from ready to produce the chair on a mass scale, but it was awesome to be considered.

"I can do that. See you next week."

Well, I'd be damned. That was about the last thing I thought my day would include when I'd gotten up that morning.

I got back to work by positioning my ladder against the house to reach the wood trim along the roofline. Years of sun and weather had rotted it in spots, and replacing it would be a relatively simple fix.

But when I was about three-fourths of the way up the ladder, the concrete sidewalk I'd set it up on cracked and gave way a few inches. Just enough to topple the ladder and send me flying to the ground.

## 32

## ESME

I'M NOT GOING TO LIE.

I cried all the way across town to the hospital when I got the call about Ty.

Matt and I had just returned from lunch, having said our goodbyes to Charli, when the call came in.

Alden was frantic and told me to come as soon as I could.

Not knowing the extent of Ty's injuries was as torturous as knowing that whatever had happened to him, had happened while he was working on my house. My shithole of a house, for which he was getting paid a pittance for his time.

How fucked was that?

What if… what if he didn't make it? His parents would have lost two children. How could they survive that?

How would *I* survive losing him?

Of course, it was supremely selfish to think of myself. I'd known Ty for such a short period of time. But I couldn't help it.

In fact, I didn't know what I would do if I lost any of the guys.

Holy shit.

Why was this just now occurring to me?

With Eddie coming around unsuccessfully to get back in my good graces, and now Ty's accident, it was like a cloud had lifted and I could finally see.

And what I saw scared and thrilled me in equal measures.

I'd grown to care about the guys more than I'd realized or wanted to admit. I mean, sure they're hot as hell and beyond generous to be working on my house when I couldn't pay them what they deserved. But now that I thought about losing one—or all—of them, well, I could barely breathe.

Once at the hospital, I ran through the corridors to the waiting room where Alden had told me to meet him. I ran straight into his arms.

"How… how is he?" I sobbed.

I was embarrassed by my emotions, but there was no holding back.

Alden put his hands on my shoulders to look at me. "We think he's going to be fine."

Oh my god.

I reached into my bag for a tissue, and that's when I realized Case was standing right next to me.

"Oh, Case," I said, embracing him.

In spite of all that was going on, I knew I needed to clear the air with him.

"Case, I realize you saw Eddie and me kissing this morning."

Alden's eyebrows shot up.

"He came to see me, asking to get back together. His kiss caught me off guard. But I've already told him to forget it. He and I are over. Done. I'm sorry you had to see that."

He nodded. "I shouldn't have jumped to conclusions. It's all good."

I took his hand and squeezed it. "Has anyone called Ty's parents?"

Case nodded. "They're on their way."

"So what happened?" I asked, holding my breath.

Alden rubbed his hand over his head. "He fell off a ladder. The ground underneath it gave way just enough to throw him off. He was knocked unconscious."

"It might not be much more than a concussion.

They're trying to figure that out now." Case's voice broke, and I held his hand tighter.

We took seats with me in the middle, holding each of the guys' hands. No one spoke.

And the ironic thing was that I had so much to say, I didn't know where to start. So I didn't.

Fortunately, a doctor joined us in the waiting room and broke the silence.

I was the first on my feet. "How's Ty? Is he going to be okay?"

The doctor patted my arm and smiled. "He'll be fine."

I clamped a hand over my mouth to stifle another sob while Case and Alden high-fived each other.

"Can… can we see him?" I asked.

"You sure can. But he has a pretty bad headache, so please speak quietly and remain calm." He led the way.

"Oh, Ty," I said, running across the darkened room and throwing my arms around his waist.

"Esme," he said in a croaky voice.

Case offered him a fist bump. "How're you feeling, buddy?"

Ty reached for his water and took a small sip. "Like I have the world's worst headache. Seriously, I'd cut my head off if I could." He laughed weakly.

I took that as a good sign.

"Guess I got pretty lucky. I have a busted up left ankle, but aside from my head, that's the worst of it."

While the guys were recapping the accident, I was trying to figure out how to put my feelings into words. I had things to say. Important things.

Ty reached for my hand. "Hey, what's up with that article on my family? I'll help you with it, Esme. I don't want you putting your job on the line for me. I really have nothing to lose when it comes down to it. I don't give a shit what people know about me."

Jesus. There he was, laid up in the hospital, worrying about *me*.

I shook my head hard. "There is no article. I'm not doing it, and I don't care if I lose my job. You are more important to me than work. All of you are," I said, looking each of them in the eye.

Ty gave a half-hearted smile and winced. "Are you sure?"

"Yup. I know what my priorities are. And they are you. All of you."

Now I had their attention.

I continued before Ty's parents arrived or we got kicked out of his room. Or both. "I… I want to accept your offer. I want to be with you. All of you. I want more of your wild, messy love. I don't know where this will go—none of us do—but I'm willing to find out, and I hope you are too. If you'll have me."

For an agonizing moment, they looked around the room, at their feet, and then at each other.

Shit. This was not going how I'd hoped it would.

Until Alden spoke. "Are you kidding? Of course, we'll have you."

I exploded with a shriek that was sure to get us kicked out of Ty's room.

Alden picked me up and twirled me around the room, and when he put me down, Case planted a huge kiss on my mouth. Not to be outdone, Ty extended his hand to me and pulled me in for a passionate kiss.

We turned around to see the nurse come in, initially hesitating when she saw me kissing and hugging all three of the guys.

I guess there'd be more of that, and I'd better prepare for it. Most people weren't going to know what to think of us.

But that was okay.

My phone buzzed, and I saw it was Matt. Adam was probably looking for me. Dammit.

"Now that I've dropped my news on you guys, believe it or not, I have to get back to work. But I'll see you this evening, okay?"

I floated back to my car, unable to wipe the smile from my face.

Ty was going to be okay, and the guys wanted me. *Me.*

How did I get so damn lucky?

But as I got closer to the office, my cozy happiness started to wither, and to make matters worse, when I'd tried to return Matt's call, I only got his voicemail.

I was going to have to tell Adam that the story he wanted so badly was not going to happen. No fucking way, no matter what he threatened me with.

I tried to breathe through the acid-y pit in my stomach. But hey, I'd handled worse. If he fired me, so be it. I'd go out and find something better.

I planned to slip back into my cube without being noticed, but the office was buzzing with excitement, unusual for a weekday afternoon.

## 33

ESME

MATT GESTURED WHEN HE SAW ME, AND I HEADED
straight for him.

"How's Ty? He going to be okay?" he asked.

I let out a long breath. "He'll be fine. Thank god.
Hey, were you trying to reach me? I tried to call you
back but—"

"Adam's gone."

Huh?

"What? What do you mean? Did something happen
to him?" I asked.

Matt shook his head. "He's gone as in fired. I guess
there were just too many complaints against him."

My mouth dropped open and it was a moment before I could respond. Had Ty made good on his promise to get rid of Adam? "You're… joking," I stammered.

He smiled. "It's true. It's the goddamn truth."

Holy crap. It was like in the Wizard of Oz when the bad witch died. You wanted to jump up and down and sing.

But gloating was ugly. So I kept my joy to myself.

The other folks in the office were not so restrained.

"The owners of the paper will be here"—he looked at his watch— "in thirty minutes."

This was some crazy shit.

"Who's going to be in charge, then?" I asked.

"Yours truly," he said, beaming. "And I'm thinking of making you the second in command. That is, if you are interested."

I couldn't recall ever having had such a crazy day. Apart from being left at the altar, that is.

I drummed my fingers on my desk. "Well, I'd have to think about that. I mean, having you as my new boss is freaky enough. But how do I know you won't stick me with shit like planning staff retreats and such?"

I bit my lip to keep from laughing. Like I'd even consider turning down the job.

Matt dropped his head back and exploded with his usual roar. When he caught his breath, he wiped a drop of sweat off his forehead. "There won't be any damn retreats. In fact, the one you've been working on can be canceled. That will be your last task related to this bullshit. If that's okay with you, that is."

"Oh my god, Matt. Congratulations. And of course, I'll be your deputy. It's… it's an honor."

"You know, you'll be getting a raise, too. Maybe you'll be able to afford that house of yours after all," he said grinning.

Holy shit. If I didn't know better, I'd think Matt was purposely giving me a leg up so I could improve my situation.

And I'd be forever grateful to him for it.

Crap. I'd just left the guys, and now I was desperate to talk to them.

Could it really be that I might be able to afford the mortgage on the house? And that I could potentially stay in it, improving it, little by little?

I needed to call my dad.

And Charli.

But I had to finish my day at the office and hear what the paper's owners were up to.

Then, straight to the hospital to see the guys.

I had news. Big news. And they were going to be thrilled for me.

Because I was theirs.

And they were mine.

## 34

ESME

"Case, I'm on my way back. Don't leave."

"Is everything okay?" he asked. "Did you have that talk with your boss about the Ty story?"

I jogged to my car. "Everything is fine. Actually, everything is great. I'll be there in a few."

Poor Case. I could see it now. He'd jump to the conclusion that I'd been fired by Adam. He'd tell the other guys, and they'd look at me sadly when I came in. They might already be talking about ways to cheer me up and help me out.

Because they cared about me.

But my good news might let me do something nice

for them, for a change. If what Matt promised was true, I'd no longer be living on ramen noodles and shopping at thrift stores.

Actually, I loved ramen noodles and thrift stores. Those two things were going nowhere.

So what would change with my new job and raise?

Pretty much nothing except that I might be able to afford the house I lived in.

I had so much to tell Charli. But that would have to wait. Same with Dad.

When I arrived, I ran down the hospital corridor just like I had earlier, passing the staff I'd seen before, who did a double take.

When I got to Ty's room, I was breathless.

"Esme," Alden said, throwing his arms around me, "you just missed Ty's parents."

My mouth dropped open, and we all turned to Ty. "Yeah? How'd it go?"

He removed the cool cloth from his eyes and squinted at us. Poor guy. "Better than I thought. My dad wants to invest in me. Help me get my furniture produced."

No. Fucking. Way.

My eyes filled with tears. Again.

"Oh, Ty, that's amazing."

He tried to smile. "I know," he said, his voice cracking. "I'll be naming the company after my sister."

Then he cleared his throat hard, the way guys did when they wanted to cover up their emotions.

Why did they always do that?

"What does that mean for McKinney Construction?" I asked, sneaking a glance at Case.

A nurse stuck her head in Ty's room. "Let's wrap it up, people. Your friend needs his rest. You can socialize when he's better."

"We're just about done," Alden called after her.

"Well, we haven't talked about this yet," Ty said, looking at Case, "but I'd like to invest in the company, Case. Help you guys get out of debt so you can properly grow."

Case's eyes bugged out. "Are you serious? Bro, you don't have to do that. You have things to spend your money on."

Ty shook his head slightly. "I know I have things to spend my money on. And McKinney Construction is one of them."

Case looked down at his feet, shaking his head. When he was ready to look at us again, he was beaming.

Like, seriously beaming.

Jesus, was he going to cry now, too?

"You're crazy, man," Case said.

Ty reached for my hand. "Esme, did you have something to tell us? Please don't say you got fired from the paper."

I bounced up and down in my sneakers, giggling. "After I hung up with Case, I realized you guys probably thought I was coming over because I'd lost my job."

Alden grimaced. "And...?"

"Quite the contrary. You won't believe this, but when I got back to the office, Adam had been fired. My friend Matt is now editor-in-chief, and...." I paused to look at each of the guys, "he's making me his second in command."

Case picked me up and swung me around the room. "That's fucking incredible. So, you're not getting fired, you don't have to do the story on Ty's family, you're getting a promotion—"

I cut him off. I couldn't help it. "And a *raise*," I squealed. "Matt said he's getting me a raise. I might be able to stay in the house."

Okay, now I was *really* jumping up and down.

"That's amazing, baby," Ty said, pulling my hand to his lips and kissing it.

"Esme, we haven't told you all of our good news," Case said.

"What? There's more?" I asked.

What else could there possibly be? Things were so perfect.

"I offered to let Alden run the company while I finish my degree," he said.

Alden nodded, smiling. "The competitors tried to lure me over, but I just couldn't do it."

"That is just incredible."

Everyone looked a little dazed, like they couldn't believe their good fortune. Of course, I was choking back tears.

So I decided to lighten the moment.

I looked at Case guiltily. "Does that mean I have to finish *Infinite Jest*?"

He dropped his head back and laughed. "You know, I've never kicked anyone out of my book club, but I think I may start with you."

He put his arms around me and ruffled my hair.

Holy shit. How could there be so much perfection in one day?

How could there be so much perfection in *one room*?

I looked at my guys, each having worked hard to pursue what they wanted, and they looked back at me, equally proud.

It seemed dreams really could come true.

I was hugging and kissing the guys yet again when the nurse returned. She stood in the doorway with her hands on her hips, trying to look mean.

She didn't fool any of us.

She smiled. "C'mon guys. You have to leave now. You're going to get me in trouble."

I grabbed my bag and planted a quick kiss on Ty's

cheek. "Okay. Okay. We're out of here. Be back tomorrow, sweetie."

Case and Alden did the guy handshake thing with Ty, and we hustled out the door with me holding each of their hands, heading into the night and into our new lives.

Did you like *Her Dirty Builders*? Learn about the next book in the Men at Work series,
*Her Dirty CEOs*

**I hope you loved reading this book as much as I loved writing it. Please visit my store to learn more about my books, and to buy directly from me!**
**https://mikalaneshop.com/**

SHOP
Mika
Lane

Dear Reader:

I'm USA TODAY bestselling romance author Mika Lane, and am OBSESSED with bringing you sassy, steamy stories with imperfect heroines and the bad-a*s dudes they bring to their knees. I'll always bring you my signature humor and heat, topped off with a modern-day happily ever after.

My first book ever was *The Day I Ate the Milkyway,* a true fourth-grade masterpiece illustrated with crayons and bound with construction paper and glue. Nowadays, steamy romance gives purpose to my days and nights as I create worlds and characters that tickle the imagination. I live in magical Northern California with my own handsome alpha dude, sometimes known as Mr. Mika Lane, and two devilish cats named Chuck and Murray.

A dual citizen of the United States and Ireland, I have on more than one occasion spent my last dollar on a plane ticket somewhere, and am always planning my next escape. I often try new recipes on unsuspecting friends, search out hiding places to read undisturbed, and sadly kill every houseplant I bring home.

I LOVE to hear from readers when I'm not dreaming up naughty tales to share. Visit my online shop https://mikalaneshop.com/ and say hello https://mikalaneshop.com/pages/meet-mika.

xoxo, Mika

www.ingramcontent.com/pod-product-compliance
Lightning Source LLC
Chambersburg PA
CBHW011150190726
48288CB00010B/3258